Shuckstack Mountain

David Henry

A novel.

Copyright 2018

One evening just before summer arrived in that year of the crash and the vagrants, the rain began. It started as all rain did, slapping loudly against the tin roof of the farm house, but it quickly became something more than a normal shower. The windows began to shake in their frames and the rain fell in sheets, each wave discernible and seemingly larger than the last. The cows made sounds like screams from their barn, but Samuel's mother assured him that they were fine.

"That barn is strong and new. Nothing to worry about. It'll take a lot more than a storm to bring it down."

"What about the other barn?"

Samuel's mother didn't respond, but only looked out the window and kept her knitting needles moving, clacking and clacking. The answer was obvious in her silence. It was not prepared to stand up to anything like this storm. As if in answer to the question that hung in the air, Tom Meller appeared at the foot of the stairs, pulling on a heavy, hooded coat. He was already wearing his thick boots.

"Your father will take care of things," Mrs. Meller said, her faux calm not quite convincing enough for an eleven year old.

"I need Samuel with me."

"Out of the question. Why just this after-"

"Blynne, I need him. It's for my own safety and the others. I'll keep him close, but we need a young pair of eyes. Come on, Samuel. Get on your boots and your coat and hurry."

Samuel dressed more quickly than he ever had in his life. This was a moment of excitement at last. The farm so rarely gave him anything to get excited about, but here his moment had come. His father spoke to him as Samuel pulled on his boots and began to lace them.

"You're gonna be our spotter. If you see anything we need to know about, you shout and you shout loud."

"What am I looking for?"

"Anything that might cause loss of life or limb. This wind will take that barn to the ground if we don't brace it."

For a moment only, Samuel allowed the horrible possibility of the barn's collapse to interrupt his excitement. Any men huddled inside would surely die. An image of a corncob pipe rolling through a puddle crossed his mind and disappeared just as quickly as it had come.

"Come on, Samuel. We have to go."
When Samuel and his father got to the old barn, the men were already roused, soaked to their bones in whatever clothes they had mustered to battle the elements. Eddard Morley, pipe unlit but clutched between his teeth as a unit of power, approached Tom Meller, bracing himself as he walked against the wind.

"We need to brace it."

"I felled a number of trees for the lofts in the new barn a few months ago. Quarter mile into the south wood They'll answer if we can manage in time."

Without removing the pipe from his mouth, Eddard Morley whistled through his teeth so that Samuel's ears ached. The vagrant men rallied to him, walking slowly through the pounding rain, looking for all the world like men possessed of an evil spirit. Samuel was to always be at hand, but out of the way. As a group of the men tramped into the woods, Samuel followed from twenty feet East. He had initially thought to stay behind with the men who were watching the barn, but his father stopped him.

"No, Samuel. With us. You can do nothing to help back there."

The trees Tom Meller had felled were exactly where he had left them. There had been little rain up to this point, and they looked as if they had not truly rotted yet. That would be crucial. The job of de-branching the felled trees had never been finished, as they had not in the end become necessary for the lofts, but it provided the men with some handles to hold. It took ten men to pull the massive trees through the woods, all of the detritus on the forest floor and the rapidly forming puddles doing no favors to their work. All in all, four trees began to slowly make their way back towards the farmland and the old barn, as long as it was still standing. The rain pounded all the while, never slowing or letting up for even a moment. The wind was so fierce at moments that Samuel was forced to hold onto a nearby tree to keep himself upright. The men dragging the trees had no such respite. Samuel noticed that many of them in the front of the line had their eyes closed, not even looking where they were going. Their bodies were bent forward, trusting to other senses that the job would be completed. In the middle of the largest tree was Eddard Morley. Samuel observed him from the distance of twenty to thirty feet. His pipe was resolutely clenched in his mouth, and his eyes were wide open against the lashing rain. They were a remarkably light blue and had the mark of cataracts that Samuel was too young to yet recognize. He was one of the few vagrants who had any heavy coat. The ill-suited wool was buttoned up to his chin. As the men struggled, and Samuel followed along, his eyes peeled for any sign of danger greater than the obvious. At one point, he believed that it had begun to hail, but it was only a cacophony of leaves being forced from their branches by the sheer power of the rain. It was disorienting, the dark green flatness of the leaves falling in his face along with the continued pounding of the rain. It was unlike anything Samuel had experienced before. He was nine years old, invincible, and living a moment he would remember forever. There wasn't likely to be another moment like this on the farm any time soon. He would need to remember this when things got particularly boring.

It was when the men had crossed the threshold from the south woods and back onto flat ground that things really began to get dicy. The ground had so deteriorated in their relatively brief absence, that every step brought the slipping of several men, and the trees themselves were soon coated in mud and thrice as heavy as they had once been. It was truly slow-going across a short span of ground that Samuel could have walked across in a few short seconds. Eventually, the men dropped the trees in place, two on each side of the barn, which miraculously still stood. It was being pushed about by the wind and the sounds of the old boards creaking were violent and jarring to the ear. Some men who had been dragging the trees near collapsed in exhaustion. Those who had stayed behind took their place as they began to move the trees into place so that they could prop them against the barn. Samuel could see but not hear his father, who was shouting at a group of men to follow him. They soon returned with shovels and began to attempt to make some kind of dent in which the trees could rest. Their shovels brought up nothing but water for a long time, but eventually they must have struck something like ground, as they began to furiously wave their arms for the others to hurry. The diggers hurried to the other side of the barn to make room for another brace. Samuel watched as the men nearest to him heaved the first tree into place. It looked to him as they finished that the tree had fallen into the barn gently, and was resting just beneath the roof in a moment of unusual serendipity. It did not at all appear as if it had been the work of a great struggle to get the tree to rest thus.

On the other side of the barn, something was wrong. Samuel saw a tree fall into sight and he ran to see what had happened. It was immediately clear that the hole had not been deep enough, the the tree had slipped, falling onto its side. Tom Meller and others were frantically picking the tree up again. Samuel saw, as the tree was brought airborne again, one man had stopped working. He was standing alone in the rain looking at where the tree had fallen. Samuel followed his line of sight and saw why the man froze so. There was a mangled body, only barely visible from the puddle in which it had fallen, been crushed into, but it was unmistakable and unmoving. A few other men paused to look, but there was nothing to be done right that moment. The man was gone. Samuel felt himself getting hot, despite the cold rain, and he felt his head begin to rise from his neck. In his shock, he was unable to recognize that he was about to vomit, and he retched down his coat front, standing still, taken by surprise by his own body. Again and again he retched, until his body only heaved and convulsed, producing nothing with the process.

He looked up, dazed and weak, and saw Eddard Morley looking at him. Two of the three trees were in place, and the barn was looking steadier against the lashing wind. Eddard took his pipe out of his mouth and tucked it into his coat pocket. He took a step towards Samuel. It all went black for the young boy.

Three months earlier.
1
Samuel Meller was nine, but he felt as if he had the weight of the world on his shoulders, if not the world, at least the state of Ohio. More and more, his father spoke to him about the future of their farm, and how Samuel ought to be more serious in his duties.

"I'm getting on in age, Samuel. I need you to understand that."

"I understand."

"It doesn't seem that way to me, or your mother." Samuel's mother looked up from her knitting in the corner, a look of irritation on her face that she had been brought into the quarrel. It was a cold night, unusually so for March, and there was a fire in the grate, though it was mostly embers as bedtime approached for the whole house. Farmhouses hit the hay early, which was always good for Samuel, as he liked the solitude of the house when his parents were asleep.

"I don't understand. I do everything you ask."

"You hate it. You get through them as quick as you can so you can go pretend to be *pastoral*, or whatever it is you do."

"What difference does it make what I do with my own time?"

"Hell of a lot of difference to me. Takes commitment to run a farm. Can't have your head be somewhere else when the hard years strike and it'd be easier to cut and run."

"Why not cut and run then?"

Samuel's mother drew in a sharp breath; her needles ceased clicking. The fire crackled ominously behind Tom Meller's face. It was a face that had been hardened by years of labor under the sun. It did not often smile, and was perfunctory even when it did.

"Do you mean to deliberately shame me?"

"Of course not, but if it's easier to sell then why not sell?"

Samuel would not understand men like his father for many more years, and he would eventually come to regret this exchange, but his core philosophy remained the same. He could not understand his father's stubborn insistence on being a farmer. There were so many things a man could be, why not try on something new for size?

"Your grandfather died on this land. Your sister died on this land before she was old enough to crawl. Your mother and I have poured our own blood into this soil. This is Meller ground. Do you understand that, boy? Our blood has nourished this ground for generations, and you offer it up for nothing more than something easy? You shame me, and you shame your mother. You may be only nine, but you're old enough to know better than this."

Tom Meller turned away just then, and tended to the fire, though it needed no tending. Samuel could not see the tears on his father's face, running down the hardened lines, but his mother's were there in plain sight, easy enough to spot even in the flickering light of the fire.

Samuel mounted the stairs his grandfather had sawn with his own hands with a quietude unusual for a fourteen year old boy. He somberly made his way to his corner bedroom with the window that overlooked the south wood of the farmland. It was in those woods that Samuel first saw a creature die. His father had shot the animal, and his mother had made it into meals for many weeks. His father had not allowed him to look away as he cut the animal's throat. The blood pooled and soaked into the ground while the young boy looked on, horrified and uncertain why such a ritual was necessary to "make him a man." It was only another example of a disconnect between Tom and Samuel Meller that would only grow as the years went on.

Samuel did not leave home that night, but it was the first time that he gave it serious thought. Staring longingly at the homeless and the vagrants had been a child's imaginings. For the first time, Samuel began to think of leaving home as a concrete matter, a possibility that might become a reality. He looked out at those woods that night, those woods he knew so well, and he imagined an escape route. A mile deep was an abandoned set of tracks, they'd not been used since before the Civil War, but his grandfather, when Samuel was just a boy of five, had told him the tracks still lead to a station somewhere.

"That's the thing about tracks," the old man had said. "They always lead somewhere."

The old man had died only a year later, never living long enough to realize just how much he had affected his grandson's life. For much of his young life, Samuel's imagined escapes had always involved following the train tracks all the way past the Meller property line and down to somewhere better, bigger, wilder.

Samuel's ninth year turned out to be a very bad year for most people. The markets crashed and there were more vagrants than ever before coming through town, lounging at store fronts, and congregating wherever it was that they could find space to sleep and be safe from the rain. There were rumors that a whole mess of them had camped out in the south woods on the Meller property.

"Sure about that, Del?" Tom Meller had said while his son stood quietly behind him.

"Just telling you what I hear, Tom."

"Christ Jesus."

Young Samuel immediately thought of his view of the woods from his window. He imagined it as it was when the sun was going down behind the trees. At that time of day, any creature that stood at the treeline was seen in a defining silhouette. Samuel imagined masses of men standing at the treeline, looking longingly up at his window, his warm bed, and his free standing home.

"Thanks for the heads up, Del."

There was an argument between Samuel's parents that night.

"He's just a boy, Tom."

"Blynne, he's nearly a man. You want him to still be a boy, but that doesn't mean he is."

"You don't need him to go with you."

"No I don't. But he needs to come with me. He needs to learn what it is to deal with a problem like an adult."

Samuel found himself walking into the south wood with his father the following morning just after sunrise, as if they were going on a hunting trip. In a way, they were. Tom Meller had his shotgun over his shoulder with some extra shells in his bird pockets. They walked in silence at first, only the sound of their boots on the crinkling leaves and needles of the forest floor greeted them. It was too early yet for even the earliest of birds. It was not until they had been walking for an hour or more, miles into the woods, that they heard the first calls.

"Did I ever tell you how this land came into the family, Samuel?"
"No, dad."
"It was a long time ago, and things were different."
Your great grandfather was playing cards with his neighbors on the very covered porch on which I nap on

Sunday afternoons. At the time, it wasn't Meller land. It was owned by a negro by the name of Lancaster. Your grandfather was having a hell of a down day, nearly losing everything he had, and I don't just mean what he showed up with that day. He had lost just about everything he and his wife had ever owned. The later into the night they played, the worse the situation became for your grandfather. He saw he and his wife living on the street, begging for food or fare on a train that might take them somewhere else. As the evening faded into night, the negro who owned the land suggested that they call it a night, that they all go to bed.

"No, I don't think so," another man said, a friend of your grandfather's. "I think we ought to keep playing. We ain't quite finished yet."

This wasn't a request, son. You understand me? Samuel understood. The men kept playing and your grandfather began to win. He began to win every hand and the negro man began to lose every hand. Soon enough, the tables had turned and it was your grandfather who had everything, and the negro had lost everything, including his farm of more than a hundred acres on which we walk.

"Great grandpa stole this farm?"

"Yes he did."

"Are the...the other man's family still around?"

"He left town pretty quickly. He was liable to get lynched otherwise."

"Shouldn't we give the farm back then?"

"Of course we should, but who'd we give it to? There's no one come to claim it."

"Then why tell me that story?"

"I thought you ought to know, Samuel. That's all. I thought you ought to know."

Father and son walked deep into the south woods on the Meller land, making their way towards where the rumor mill suggested the hard luck vagrants were camping out. Samuel followed his father unquestioningly, although he knew without a doubt a better, faster way to get to where they were going. It was what counted as a valley on the relatively flat Meller land. It was at the bottom of a hill, and had once been a dumping ground for railroad junk. There were rail ties and other bits of twisted iron lying about, rusted to nought by years of exposure, but with no one willing to expend the effort to rid the woods of their presence. At the bottom of this hill among the railroad refuse was a group of ten or so ragged-looking men. A few smoked home-rolled cigarettes, some slept with their hats over their faces, still other rooted around in the dirt with sticks, unable to remain still for too long. Slowly, their tired, worn faces turned up to see Samuel and his father standing in their midst. The shotgun remained on Tom's shoulder, but its presence was felt. Some of the men stood up or pushed themselves up to sitting positions against their tree trunks. One man spit on the ground and chewed on a piece of dead sawgrass. Tom Meller spoke his piece with a dignity that aroused pride in Samuel's heart. Samuel was not often moved to feel anything towards his father, but this was a rare occasion where Tom showed himself to be more than just a hardened farmer, worn thin by years of labor and personal loss.

"Tom Meller's my name, and this is my son Samuel. This is my property you're on here."
A few men made as if to scurry, but Tom put his hand up to stop them.

"I'm not here to ask you to leave or to run you off. I'm here to offer you an opportunity. This land you're on isn't just woods. I've a farm that's doing well at the moment. In a few months time it'll be detasseling season and I'll need as much help as I can get. In the meantime, I can offer you my old barn as a roof over your head. It doesn't house any animals since three years past when I built the new barn, but it still smells like hell. There's holes in the roof and mud puddles tend to form in the middle. But there's lofts and I can provide hay and some blankets. Anyone here who wants to take me up on it will be welcome, provided he doesn't cause any trouble. I reckon you can find your own way. That's about all I've come to say. Come on, Samuel."

Tom lead his son by the hand back up the hill, and towards their home. Samuel was dying to ask more questions about the provenance of their farm, but it was clear that topic was finished for the day. It would be many years before Samuel was able to go down that path again.

3

The men did not all show up, but some decided to take their chances on this Tom Meller fellow. He'd acquitted himself well in their presence. He had been firm, but kind. He did not insult the intelligence or the manhood of any of the vagrants, but treated them with at least a modicum of respect. It wasn't charity he was offering, but dignity, and it wasn't free. Slowly they trickled in from the south wood, appearing in twos or threes and knocking gently on the kitchen door. Each time, Tom would have Samuel's mother bring them a cold glass of water and some biscuits. He would sit down with them on the back porch and discuss all of the potential ways they could be needed around the farm. There was no discussion of payment and there was no formal agreement. They were free to go whenever they pleased, but as long as they were going to stay, they were going to work. The men were quiet, grateful for the biscuits, and deferential, offering little more than one word answers or nods.

There was one man who bucked that trend. Samuel had listened in from the stairs, and had even peeked around the corner one time to get a look at the man with the gravelly voice. He was dirty, but less so than the others, as if he'd made some attempts to tidy himself in spite of his situation. He sat up straight as a rod and kept his hands folded in front of him like he was praying. A corn cob was thrust in his shirt pocket, and he smelled of sweet tobacco smoke, even from Samuel's distance.

"Why would you ask that?" Tom said. "Have I not offered you enough?"

"You've offered plenty. More than necessary. I meant you no offense, Mr. Meller. I was only recalling what you said about the barn roof. I'm a fair hand if you can spare the lumber."

The man was offering to repair the barn roof so that it wouldn't rain on himself or the other vagrants.

"I'll see what I can do about some lumber and some roofing nail."

"Eddard," the man said. Taking Mr. Meller's outstretched hand in a shake. "Eddard Morley."

Around town there were whispers about what Tom Meller was doing out at his place, housing all those vagrants, offering those criminals a warm bed to sleep at night. Some folks said he was fixing to use them as some kind of personal security force around his property, despite the fact that the Mellers had never much cared about the occasional trespasser, so long as they kept to themselves. A few women were willing to offer him the benefit of the doubt and suggest that he was being a good christian.

"Well I think we ought to make sure that's what he's doing, don't you sheriff?"
Ted Fribley was the town malcontent, a handyman by trade, though as Tom Meller said to Del on occasion, "he's neither very much handy or very much of a man."

"I'm not a man to slander another man's good christian charity, but in the interest of the women and children, we should make sure that the situation out at the Meller place is under control."

"It's his own property," Sheriff Meyer said. "Who am I to tell him what he can and can't do with his old barn?"

With that, the sheriff left the hardware store by the front door, not taking any care to make sure it didn't slam behind him and in the face of Ted Fribley. Friedrich Meyer liked Tom Meller. When Friedrich had moved to town, there had been all sorts of whispers about "the new kraut sheriff" sent to spy on them for the Germans. Tom had stuck up for him, suggesting the obvious: "The hell do the Germans care about Ohio? Tell you what I do know, I hear they know their way around a keg of beer. How's that rumor hold up, Meyer?"

Tom had helped Sheriff Meyer set up a garden party on the Meller property and the sheriff had made sure a few kegs of German beer made it to the lawn, and all was forgiven, or at least forgotten for awhile. Meyer had *never* forgotten and could not bring himself to believe that Tom was doing anything unseemly. Still, he made a note to go and pay the Meller place a visit to see just what was going on out there.

Samuel watched the vagrant men from afar but with great interest. Most of Samuel's duties were related to either his own self-sufficiency or the dairy side of the farm. His was a world in which he was intentionally cloistered from the potential danger of interaction with the men who lived in the old barn. He had watched from his milking stool, losing his concentration and nearly being kicked in the face by Martha the cow while Eddard Morley patched the roof on the old barn. "Damn near doing me a favor is he," Samuel's father would say later. Samuel watched as the man did his work, holding extra roofing nails between his teeth, another hammer looped in his work pants. Morley was shirtless and shining with sweat. His body was a deep tan color that did not match the earliness of the season. Coarse, silver hair reflected the afternoon sun off his chest. He worked with the kind of diligence that Tom

Meller could appreciate, the kind of diligence he wished his son would show from time to time.

Morley was getting on in years, too old most would say, to be doing roofing work, but Samuel was struck by the beauty of the old man's body. It was not a sexual urge that Samuel was feeling. He was too young to have felt that in any capacity just yet, but he felt a startling sense of reverence watching the old man work. He had the beauty of a gnarled oak tree in its last decade of many, wounded but determined to live the remainder of its time with dignity and allow some of its former strength and glory to shine through in its final moments. It did not occur to Samuel at such a young age how this view of Eddard might have been insulting, condescending even. He was enraptured by the man's presence on the farm, but could not invent any way for their paths to cross. He was forced for some time to observe the figure from afar, perhaps adding to the mythical proportions in which Samuel held him in his mind. From the screen porch on the front of the farmhouse, Samuel saw the old man pulling weeds with the rest of the men, only he wasn't pulling anything. While the rest of the men bent over and stretched out their hands to pluck weeds from the ground, the old man carried a scythe at his side, gently nicking the weeds at their root and leaving them lying dead atop the grass. After some time, another man would come by and notice the pile and collect them. All the while, Eddard Morley remained erect and walking with dignity that none of the other men could muster.

Once, from his bedroom window, he saw Eddard directing the other men in a game of baseball. He sat on a stump, pipe in the side of his mouth, and pointed with his arms, extending a long middle finger to point. Distance and windowpane prevented Samuel from hearing any words from the old man's lips, but he saw the look of rapt attention on the other men's faces as they stopped what they were doing to pay attention to Eddard Morley. Samuel watched the baseball game with enjoyment, cheering along in his room as if he was listening to the Cardinals on the radio. It was unclear who was on what team, with men switching back and forth at all times, but everyone was having a grand time. Once, Eddard Morley slapped his knees in uncontrolled mirth and fell backwards off the stump on which he sat, still laughing as another man ran to offer him a hand up from the ground. All of the men looked more complete during the game, as if while they were picking weeds or chopping wood, or lounging about the yard, they were only half men, managing miraculously to continue until the rest of their body was able to find them.

When Samuel told his mother and father about the baseball game, he was surprised at the violence of their response. They were not upset at the men for having their fun, but at Samuel's words.

"It isn't fit to talk like that," his mother said. "They're just men like any other and that's the end of it."

"Your mother's right. You oughtn't have spied on them that way. It's inappropriate."

There was something in his parents' tone that confused Samuel. Their arguments didn't make any sense, and it seemed that they knew it. They spoke with a greater intensity and anger because they knew they weren't making any sense. If they were only men like anyone else, then why was it wrong to watch them play their game? It didn't add up.

"You are not to associate with those men," Tom Meller said firmly.

"But you talk to them just like Del or Friedrich. I've seen you. You don't treat them any different."

"I'm a man, Samuel. You're just a boy. I can afford to treat them with respect. If there's anything you should learn from these men, it's this: always give the respect you can afford, and not an iota more. I took you out into the south wood with me for a reason. I wanted you to see how to act like a man. Right now I want you to act like a boy and mind."

No matter how he thought on it, Samuel could not make any sense of his parents' words. He couldn't for the life of him understand what they were so worried about. Hadn't they seen Eddard Morley too? If any man had dignity, it was him. He didn't deserve to be among the men he was, patching barn roofs and living on another man's land. He was better than that. He was better than all of them, no matter what Samuel's parents thought about it.

The night after the afternoon baseball game was the night of the storm, the night the old barn nearly met its end, and the night that Samuel lost some of his innocence.

4

When Samuel awoke, he was lying in his own bed, his mother's face close to his own, his father a few feet away, leaning against the wall, his hands in his pockets. It was daytime, and there was sun streaming in through Samuel's bedroom window. Samuel tried to sit up, but his mother's hand gently held him down.

"Not yet dear. You've been through a great ordeal."

"That man."

"You did a good job, son," Tom Meller said.
That wasn't an answer at all to Samuel's implied question. Samuel had remembered the man. He didn't say anything about himself.

"Is he okay? The man is he okay?"
His mother would not meet his eye. His father took a deep breath before speaking again.

"He's gone, Samuel. I helped bury him this morning."

"I should have helped."

"You did enough, Samuel."

"I didn't do anything! I was supposed to make sure no one got hurt and that's exactly what happened."

"You couldn't have prevented what happened. There was nothing you could have done. That's the way things are."

"You need more rest," Mrs. Meller said.

"All I've done is rest."

"Your mother's right."

When his parents left his room, he did not go back to sleep, nor did he stay in bed. He went to his window and looked out. If he strained his neck and looked out the right side of his window, he could see the old barn and the four trees holding it in place. It didn't look quite the same. The men were mostly visible, which was unusual. Some of them milled about, a few threw a baseball, but most of them were lounging wherever they could find a spot between the puddles that dominated the landscape. Samuel could see the treeline reflected back at him hundreds of times from puddles all over. Walking among the men, stopping here and there to talk, was Eddard Morley. It was his face that Samuel had last seen before blacking out, and here he was, carrying on as ever. No one seemed particularly pleased to talk to him, but still he went from man to man, occasionally stopping to tamp down his pipe or to light it once more. Samuel would soon know what it was that Eddard Morley was doing.

It was his father who told him about the funeral service. First, his mother came by and made him put on his Sunday clothes, but she wouldn't say why, only that "your father will explain it."

"I helped dig the plot myself. Some of the men think it's a good idea to say a few words. You ought to be there."

"Is mother coming?"
"She...no."

The body was buried further into the south wood than seemed strictly necessary. Samuel could not help but imagine how difficult it must have been to carry the body such a distance. Maybe his father had wanted it to be difficult, had wanted it to take some time. The spot they had chosen was in a small clearing devoid of any unseemly detritus. The earth was still fresh, and a simple cross stood at the head of the grave. The men who chose to attend stood in a circle around the plot, and Eddard Morley stepped forward to speak. He had slicked his hair back and his piped was tucked neatly into his shirt pocket. He cleared his throat and rubbed the side of his nose before speaking.

"His name was Thomas Howell. He was thirty years old and came from Maryland. There's a wife and a small boy. Thomas had a dollar and seven cents to his name. Mr. Meller has graciously offered to pay the postage so that Mr. Howell's wife and child receive that money. Thomas Howell was known to be a fair hand at cards. Unfortunately, that was all I was able to find out about the man. He was a son of God, as all of us are. I pray that he may rest in peace."

Samuel wanted to scream. That was it? The man's life was summed up just like that? Who cared if he was good at cards? What did that have to do with anything? It was all so pathetic and haphazard. For the first time, Samuel was angry at Eddard Morley. The man failed at his duties. He was supposed to honor this man, but he hadn't done that. He'd only said a few things about him and then he'd been done.

"Come on, Samuel," Tom Meller said, holding him by the shoulders and leading him towards the house. "Let's go."

"No."

"Let's go."

"No," Samuel cried and broke free of his father's grip. He ran by the men, bumping against Eddard Morley's shoulder as he ran by. He sprinted further into the woods, running through the trees as best he could. He only stopped to catch his breath after several hundred yards. He looked back to see the men were only just visible. The speck that he imagined was his father was being comforted by another man. A hand rested on Tom Meller's shoulder. Samuel turned away and started walking.

The woods were alive with bird calls and noises without specific origin that seem to abound when the sunlight first hits the trees after a prolonged rain. The nine year old boy walked alone. It was true that Samuel had known death before. His grandparents had passed, but they had been old, and their passing had felt meaningful in the scope of time. Thomas Howell's death felt trite and useless. It was the first time that Samuel had truly felt the weight of death fall squarely on his shoulders...and he only wished it felt heavier. It was pitifully light, and that haunted him. The man had simply been snuffed out. Here, and then gone. The meaninglessness of it, and his father and Eddard Morley's pitiful attempts to give meaning to a death that had none was what angered the boy so much. He imagined any number of deaths befalling himself as he walked through the trees. There were bobcats in the woods, bears maybe, plenty of holes he could fall into and get stuck. He could leave the world at any moment and it wouldn't make a lick of difference. He had been right about that night: he would remember it forever. It had been a night of excitement and importance, but not for Thomas Howell.

Death is only important to the living. They struggle and grasp at straws to make sure it means something, anything, so that when it's their turn, someone might do the same.

5

If nothing else, the event cemented in Samuel's mind his desire to leave the farm forever, no matter what his father said. He wanted his life to mean something before he died, and he wasn't going to accomplish that by staying on the Meller plot. That much was sure. No one made any comment about Samuel's reappearance in the farm house an hour later than everyone else had returned. He was allowed to go up to his room with only cursory looks from his mother and father. His mother's lips were pursed, but in the end she said nothing. Over the next few weeks, Samuel kept mostly to himself. He got all of his work done, but it was obvious to everyone that he was truly grieving for the first time in his life. Samuel imagined that he was plotting, planning his life after leaving the farm, but he wasn't. Imagining the future is a denial of the painful present. It was his coping mechanism, and no one was willing to fault him for it.

In the early afternoons, his chores finished, Samuel would walk into the south wood, his pea shooter over his

shoulder and a few biscuits in his pocket. He wandered
mostly, shooting at squirrels and old glass bottles.
Sometimes he'd follow the old train tracks for a mile or so,
but never left the Meller property. The tracks kept going,
seemingly endlessly, but surely they had to end too.
Samuel imagined his life after the farm in a few ways.
Being a war hero was obviously the best option. In war,
death wasn't meaningless. There was a special significance
to those who had died in war for their country. Tom
Meller had fought in the great war, and although he never
talked about it, he always insisted on great reverence
whenever it was brought up. Samuel misinterpreted his
father badly in this instance. He was much too young to
understand the special, almost incomprehensibly pointless
nature of a death in war. To him, it still seemed the most
meaningful type of death. It was a child's view of the
world, and a child's imaginings of a better life, but that's all
Samuel was at this time. As he aged, his perception of the
farm would change, and his views of the world would
become more nuanced, but the stubborn, nagging feeling

of the farm not being enough for him…well that would stay.

On one of these wandering afternoons, Samuel came back into the fields and tripped, fell straight on his face. It was not until he dusted himself off that he realized he hadn't tripped on a tree root, but a man. There right at the tree line, propped up against a tree, pipe lit and smoking, was Eddard Morley. His legs were crossed and his thumb was placed in the middle of a book. His light eyes were fixed on Samuel with curiosity.

"Sorry to trip you up."

"I wasn't paying attention."

"You were walking mighty quick. Where you off to?"

"Just home. Been out walking."

Eddard Morley nodded and took a puff from his pipe as if this needed to be thought over for a moment, as if Samuel had said something of great import instead of simply admitting to walking in the woods aimlessly. An ineffable force kept Samuel's feet firmly in place, though the house was in sight. He needed to hear what Eddard was going to say.

"Took Howell's death hard didn't you?"

"What?"

"Thomas Howell. The man crushed by the tree the night of the storm. You know who I mean."

"Yeah."

"Was your job to be on the lookout wasn't it?"

"It was. I messed up."

"Maybe so."

Again, he took a puff from his pipe. As he inhaled deeply, he crossed his arms across his chest, his pipe coming out underneath the opposite armpit. He stared out over the fields. It was a quiet, early summer afternoon, the sunlight a substitution for sound.

"Well it ought to offer you some perspective I suppose."

"Perspective? It made me realize I'm leaving this place if that's what you mean."

"I'm not sure it is. But you suit yourself."

"I'm leaving. I hate it here," Samuel said as if challenged. " Nothing ever happens. I don't want to die without ever having done anything, a stupid tree snuffing me out like that."

"Foolish notion, that."

"What do you know?" Samuel said angrily. "You don't have a job or a home or anything. Why should anyone listen to you?"

"That's fair, Samuel. All those things are true. I don't have a family either. Does that prevent me from knowing yours is a pretty good one? Your father's a good man, and this is a nice farm. It'd be a right shame to throw it away out of fear."

"I'm not afraid."

"Like hell you aren't. You'd run away from this place because you don't want to be trapped here. Well I've got a secret for you: being trapped here ain't half bad. You ought to be happy you've got the chance."

With that, Samuel's one-time idol pushed himself up and walked away into the fields and back to the old barn, leaving the young boy to reckon with his words as best he could. When the chance to meet him had finally come, Eddard Morley hadn't been like what Samuel had imagined at all. In all his imaginings, Morley had told him about his epic life before the farm. He'd never talked about how great it was. In Samuel's mind, Eddard should have been upset to find himself in such a situation. Look at all he had lost! It was he who was the fool, not Samuel.

The vagrants stayed on the Meller property for more than a year. After a number of negotiations, Tom Meller had managed to convince the railroad to take them on, the whole lot of them. They weren't going to be paid a hell of a lot, but they were going to have jobs, which is more than could be said for masses of men across the country. It was a huge victory, and it was to be celebrated like one. In the time since the men had moved into the old barn, and Eddard Morley had crouched on the roof and patched the hole, the men had done a good deal more work on the old barn. It had new, permanent braces that weren't unstripped trees, an entirely new roof, and a new coat of paint on the outside. The lofts had been entirely rebuilt, piece by piece, over the course of the year. A new summer was coming on, and Tom Meller was pleased to say that he would be hiring local boys to do summer work once more, and he could even offer them a place to lodge if their mothers saw fit. As a dual celebration, there was to be a massive party in the Meller's old barn to send off the newly-minted railroad men, and to welcome another summer. The whole town was invited.

Samuel feigned indifference whenever his parents mentioned the party planning going on, rarely taking the time to look up from whatever book he was reading. He had taken to reading with a fever of recent, and particularly to the journals of Thoreau, reading them again and again with a sort of religious devotion.

"Trees are the closest thing I have to religion," he said one day aloud at the dinner table.
Blynne Meller stood up and slapped her son across the face, leaving an angry red welt on his cheek.

"The Lord Jesus Christ ought to be first in your heart. I'll hear no more of it."

"No, ma'am," he said quietly, not wanting his Thoreau to be taken away.

Samuel's words were true though. His solemn, mourning walks in the woods after the death of the vagrant Howell had changed in character. While his walks had initially been plans of leaving, ways of ignoring the very concept of death, they had become communes with the south wood. What had begun aimlessly had turned into purposeful retreats from farm life. He learned from Thoreau the sanctity of the natural world, and how it provides a meaning for man. To be a steward of the natural world is his purpose, his religion, his mission. Whenever man might impose on that sacred duty, he ought to be opposed mightily, although nonviolently. Twelve year old Samuel began to privately refer to himself as a pacifist, and he even asked Del if there were any books he could get him about Buddhism.

"Sammy I've not ordered any like that before, and I don't reckon your parents would like it much."

"I'll pay you extra," Samuel said, pleading in his eyes.

"Why not another Thoreau journal? You've got what, Fall and Summer? Four seasons you know."

"You really won't, Del?"

"It's not about the money. I'd need to hear it from your parents. I don't mind ordering books for you, but this is something different."

Samuel eventually dropped it, stopped asking Del to order him books that could directly be used to criticize him. Del had no problem ordering Whitman or Emerson or even Marx, because the shopkeeper didn't have a clue who the men were, and he happily ordered them, thinking that the Meller's had a real scholar on their hands. Samuel devoured the books, reading them over and over until their cheap bindings wore out and all that kept them together were his own folded hands. He read atop logs and with his back against trees. He read with his legs crossed in front of him on mossy ground near a creek, and he read sitting comfortably between old railroad slats. There was hardly a space large enough to contain him comfortably in the south wood where he had not imbibed of the sweet nectar of literature that appreciated nature as much as his young heart.

6

When the day of the party arrived, a Saturday in May, Samuel considered sneaking off and skipping the whole charade. His parents had been on edge lately, and he didn't want to upset them and risk a punishment that might take away his books. Neither of his parents were very good readers, so he wasn't concerned about them reading the books, but only taking them away. He decided to attend the party, to be a good and amiable son so that he might be in their good graces again. He wore brown corduroy pants, a white shirt, and cordovan shoes that hardly ever saw the light of day. He stepped smartly out of the farmhouse just as the sun was setting. The party was to begin at dusk, but based on the steady murmuring of sounds coming from the barn, things had already gotten started. There had not been much reason to celebrate in the last year, and folks were eager to cut loose. It seemed that the whole town had been invited, and indeed RSVP'd, because there was hardly an inch of space in which to maneuver in the old barn.

Samuel spent the better part of an hour on getting from one end of the barn to the other, where the refreshments were laid out, and quickly being devoured. Samuel looked around for his parents before helping himself to some of Sheriff Meyers' beer. He saw his father, red-faced and laughing, spinning his mother on the dance floor. Samuel took his mug of beer and a piece of cake and retreated up into a loft. While the floor space was all taken, there were lofts that were still unoccupied. At least, he thought his chosen loft was unoccupied. When he pulled himself up and settled himself among the hay, Samuel realized he wasn't alone at all. Eddard Morley sat at the back of the loft, a plate with nothing but crumbs on it at his side, his pipe as ever, in his mouth. Morley and Samuel had not exchanged more than a dozen words in the year since, and Samuel had long-since ceased admiring the man as some kind of rough deity. Still, politeness was to be expected.

"No need to hide that," Eddard Morley said, inclining his head in the direction of the beer that Samuel held at his side. "It's a celebration. I'll not tell."

"Thanks." He raised his glass to the old man before taking a swig. After wiping his chin he said, "Are you excited to work on the railroad?"

"Not quite the word for it. Grateful, for certain. Your father's one of the good ones."

"You've said that before."

"Meant it. You still aiming to get out of here at first chance?"

"I could go to school."

"Your parents heard that plan?" he asked, eyes wandering towards the whirling Mellers of the dance floor.

"No."

"I don't think they'd be too opposed."

"They want me to run the farm."

"What, a farmer can't be well-read now?" Samuel took another swig of his beer, some redness coming to his cheeks and ears, the music starting to sound more appealing, more immediate. He looked across the barn and saw directly into the loft on the other side. There was a girl there who was a bit older than him, Amelia Fribley. She sat by herself, wearing a white dress and ankle frills, her hair plaited at the back, dressed up but with no one to talk to.

"What's her name?" Eddard asked.
"Who?"
"Girl across the way. What's her name?"
"Amelia Fribley."
"That jackass's daughter?"
"My father doesn't think too highly of Ted Fribley if that's what you mean."
"I think you took my meaning. Ugly name, Fribley. Doesn't fit Amelia at all does it?"
Samuel had to admit to agreeing with the old man. It didn't fit at all. In fact, she hardly fit with her father. It was almost unbelievable that she came from him. She was quiet to his boisterousness. Most around town said she was quiet as to offset her old man. Her mother had been that way too. "He's always needed someone around who he could yell at," folks said. "Poor girl."

"Hogwash," Eddard Morley said. "Her old man's a right bastard, but that's a hell of an assumption to make.

Just because he's that way doesn't mean she takes it lightly. Just means she has some dignity in public. More people ought to have such dignity. Still though, Fribley isn't any name for her."

Samuel was no longer quite sure who Eddard Morley was speaking to, or if he was the one being addressed. Still, he could not help but agree with the old man once more. He had often harbored the same thoughts about Amelia, but had never quite known how to express them out loud. Amelia Meller had a nice ring to it, much better than Fribley. Morley was right. Fribley was no name for an Amelia. But who was Samuel to tell her such a thing, a girl three years his senior, and stunning to boot. These were private thoughts.

"Should go and recite to her some of that poetry you're always reading," Eddard said suddenly.

"Pardon?"

"Beats the hell out of sitting here with me. You don't even like me."

"I don't...I don't dislike…"

"Ah forget it. All I'm saying is be true to your own philosophy, even if it's a fool philosophy. Carpe diem right?

"What?"

"You hard of hearing or what? Isn't that what you told me? You wanted to live a meaningful life before you die? Well sitting here with me is no better than farming so far as I can tell. Go and talk to the Amelia whose last name doesn't suit. The way I figure it, if you don't, you yelled at me for no damn reason."

"You're right."

"You don't sound pleased by that. Give it a shot. Just might make you a man. If nothing else, might change your philosophy. Life's been known to do that to the most rigid of philosophers."

"I'm scared."

"Of course you are. Now get out of my loft."

"Excuse-"

"I'll push, boy."

Samuel climbed down from the loft space, abandoning what was left of his beer and cake. He found, once his feet were on the floor that he felt dizzy, his legs wobbled, and the distance across the barn to the other loft was akin to a hundred miles. He put one foot in front of the other, although not always so well. He figured that eventually he would get to the other side, and the beer would help that time pass faster than it really did. It appeared that Amelia Fribley noticed his coming from a ways out, but politely pretended as if she didn't see the young man making a beeline for her presence. For all his reading of noble truths of the world and his feeling that he was beginning to understand everything and his place in it, Samuel had never been quite so frightened in his life. There was no word in Thoreau, Whitman, or the others that could have prepared him for such a moment. What good was the dying exhortations of a soldier on the battlefield to a young man tasked with speaking to a woman? How helpful would a dialect on man's relation to nature be to Samuel in this moment? The young man felt a massive hole appear in his knowledge. Always his knowledge seemed to be expanding from the center, reaching outwards to as far as he could take himself in one life, and yet...that had been wrong. His knowledge was not expanding from the center, because it was this knowledge he was lacking, right in the center of his being. He could feel it, and he was woefully unprepared to find out what might happen. And yet he went onwards to his fate.

She offered him a hand up into the loft as his foot slipped on one of the rungs. Her hand was not soft as Samuel imagined, but not truly a farmer's hand either. It was a girl's hand, but a girl who knew work. He looked up into her eyes as she helped him up and saw a familiar lightness to them. But unlike Eddard Morley, hers were not damaged. They were not light from an affliction, but of a singular beauty. She invited him to sit down next to her, patting the hay. She had a nearly empty glass of punch next to her.

"Do you need me to refill that?" Samuel asked, eager for a reason to speak.

"No thanks. That's okay. Why don't you sit down. You look a bit red about the face."

"It's hot in here."

"It is. That must be it. You're Samuel Meller aren't you?"

"Yes."

"I'm Amelia Fribley."

"I know it. I mean I don't-"

Amelia Fribley laughed at Samuel, not unkindly, but nor did she cover her face with her hand. It was simply funny, his inability to speak. She was thirteen and a little wiser, not entirely unfamiliar with the stuttering figure Samuel cut in front of her.

"Lovely party your father has thrown. The whole town is grateful."

"It's okay I guess."

"Just okay? Seems grand to me. As grand as this town knows anyhow."

This was a thread that Samuel could pick up and run with. He thought he heard an echo of his own thoughts in that of the older girl.

"What does this town know?" he said. "I can't wait to leave here. There's nothing it has to offer that I need."

"That's pretty callous."

"No I believe it. What good thing does this town have? It's plain all over. I want to live before I die."

"Do you suppose people here aren't living? Is this a gathering of corpses then? You sound silly when you talk that way, though you sound so convinced."

"I mean to leave this place when I'm old enough, if that's what you mean."

"Well I think plenty of good things come from here, and I also think plenty of good things are plain for that matter. I have plain brown hair, a very dull color, quite common. Do you think that's terrible and not worth your time? What about my teeth? Also very plain. See this one, it's out of order and cuts at my gum. You can't tell unless I show it to you, but it's there. What about me? I come from this town too. I happen to think I'm alright. I may not be the Queen of England but I'm something."

"I didn't mean all that," Samuel said.

"Then I think you ought to be a great deal more careful with your words. You'll hurt somebody's feelings going around talking like that."

"I only meant to-"

"I think I do want some more punch. Could you make room for me to get by?"

She shuffled past Samuel, careful not to rip or dirty her white dress, and when she mounted the ladder down, he spoke to her again.

"Do...you want to dance?" he asked the top of her head.

She didn't look up at him until she reached the floor.

"Not today I don't think," she said, before walking away.

Samuel looked across the barn at Eddard Morley, though his eyes were closed, his pipe resting gently on his chest. Perhaps he hadn't seen Samuel make a mess of it. He didn't know why he cared what the old man thought anyway. He was nothing but an old vagrant turned railway worker. Still.

7

Samuel's friendship with Eddard Morley began in earnest in only the last month of the old man's stay on the farm. He and the rest of the men were scheduled to leave on the rails as May turned to June of Samuel's tenth year, and the youth simply could not help himself from asking Eddard about Amelia again. Something in the way the old man had spoken of her had belied a certain knowledge, perhaps that knowledge that Samuel could now feel was missing from his center. On top of that, she had espoused similar sentiments to the old man when it came to the farm and leaving town. Maybe he could offer some help.

Samuel was not technically allowed to associate with the vagrants, although he had a feeling that rule had laxed somewhat over the course of the last year. He still did not want to push his parents' patience, and decided that he would need to ask Eddard Morley about the situation in private. Samuel began to linger by the treeline instead of walking deep into the woods with his books. He would set up only twenty or thirty feet into the south woods, propped up against a tree, not really reading, but keeping an eye out for the old man in the shifting afternoon shadows. Hadn't the old man been reading at the treeline that day when they had spoken a year before? Samuel suddenly wished he had not stopped paying attention to the comings and goings of the old man. Come to think of it, Samuel had not paid much attention to anything but his books over the last year. He wondered what else he might have missed out on. After a few days of stakeouts, Samuel's strategy paid off. He looked up from his *Bartram's Travels* and saw the old man packing his pipe, his back against a tree just like Samuel sat. He blew air between his teeth, trying to get the old man's attention. Morley went right about packing his pipe as if nothing had happened. Samuel tried again, but failed miserably once more. Finally, he picked up some small stones and began to toss them towards Eddard Morley. Once landed squarely on the man's knee and he looked up.

"Now what's that about?"
"Can you come over here?"

"I'm much older and more infirm than you, why don't you come here if you want to talk to me?"

"Please? Can you please just come here?"

Eddard Morley made a great show of how difficult it was for him to get up, though Samuel had seen with his own eyes that he lived in one of the loft spaces that required climbing a ladder. Eddard made absurd noises getting to his feet and lumbering over towards the boy, only to settle himself once more against a tree, directly across from the boy.

"Now what's this all about?"

"I'm not supposed to talk to you. Or at least I don't think I am."

"So this is some kind of secret meeting of the minds?"

"Something like that."

The old man chuckled, wheezing a little as he held his pipe between his teeth and tried to light a match. It took him a few tries, as his body shook with laughter, but eventually he got his pipe lit and shook the match out. He looked across at his young companion.

"About that girl isn't it?"
Samuel didn't respond.

"Oh yeah, I saw you fuck that right up."

"Hey I'll-"

"What? Tell your father I did something unchristian? Go right ahead, Buddhist."

"I was only gonna say I knew you were faking sleep."

"Who says it was fake? Maybe your courtship attempt put me to sleep."

"She sounded like you," Samuel said, cutting right to the point. This made the old man laugh some more.

"Courting me are you?"

"She just, I think I made her mad."

"Well that much was pretty clear from my end. What'd you do, go spouting off about how shit this town is?"

"Well, yeah. That's what I did. But I tried to explain that I want to go do something great with my life. Doesn't everybody want that?"

"You know her daddy?"

"Yeah we talked about this. Everybody knows Mr. Fribley. He's a handyman of sorts."

"Of sorts."

"So what? What's that got to do with anything?"

"You are even thicker than I thought. All those books. I'll spell it out for you then. What do you think the odds are that she gets to leave this town? Does her daddy own his own land? Can her daddy afford to send her to school if it suits her? Fribley sitting on a secret fortune? Don't you get it? She ain't leavin this town, and it'd be a damn sore way to live if she decided she hated it like you do, because she'd have to live with it all the time. She ain't going anywhere, and you shit all over her future like it wasn't nothing."

Samuel let this sink in for a moment, beginning to see just how thick he had been. He was right to come to Eddard for advice. Samuel never could have talked to his mother or father about something like this.

"Well if she was my girl, I'd take her with me. She'd get to leave here with me, wherever it was I went."

"How noble."

"Well isn't it?"

"Why don't you march over to her house right now and tell that girl's two years your senior that you're about to be her saving grace. What kind of ass do you want to make yourself out to be? I know you've got some sense in there, but you're sure not showing it right now."

"Well what do I do?"

"Now we've come straight out with it. What makes you think I know anything about it? I'm just a lonely old man."

"Have you ever been in love?"

"That what you think you are? Last I checked, you'd hardly gotten a few words out with this girl. But yes, I've been in love. I was married."

"What happened?"

"I'll tell you this," he said, tamping down his pipe and adding some more tobacco. "Only because I'm leaving in a few weeks and I won't have to feel your pity eyes on me for too long. I was married when I came here, married twenty five good years. At least twenty or so were good anyhow. I lost my job and I didn't find another one for a long, long time. I went west to find some kind of work, same as the rest of these men, and as you know we didn't find any and we ran out of money. I sent home whatever I could scrounge, but her letters became more and more vague. The divorce papers came with the longest letter yet. She'd found someone else who could take care of her. I don't blame her really. What can I offer her anymore?"

"But that's terrible. How can she do that to you?"

"There's a lot that's terrible, but still right. You'll be surprised what we can rationalize and live through. She was a right fine woman. We used to dance. Even when we ran out of money and couldn't dance in the clubs anymore, we'd crank up the radio, get dressed up and dance on our kitchen linoleum. We danced our hearts out. It's how we best expressed ourselves to each other. Shame of the letters, we couldn't really express ourselves the way we could if she'd been here to dance with me."

"You didn't dance at the party."

"No I didn't."

"I'm sorry."

"We aren't here to talk about me. That isn't what our secret meeting of the minds is about. This is about you and that girl you think you love."

"I'm sorry."

"Enough, Samuel. Know when your empathy turns to pity. Now listen to me, if you love someone don't you want to share the best things with them? Don't you want them to experience your favorite things with you?"

"Of course."

"Then why did you walk straight up to that girl and start complaining?"

"Oh."

"Oh's right. You didn't walk up there and start talking about all those long walks in the woods you love so much. You talked about how you want to leave. I'd not stick around to talk to you either."

"That makes sense."

"Seems too easy doesn't it?"

"By half."

"That's the devil of it. We always overthink it."

Over the course of Eddard Morley's last three weeks on the farm, he and Samuel met nearly every day at the same spot during the same waning, afternoon hours. Samuel's absence was not noted, because he was always out walking at those hours anyway. Samuel and Eddard spoke of love, and what Samuel should do should he be given another chance to speak to Amelia, but Eddard could not be convinced to speak of his wife anymore. It was painful to Samuel to learn such a thing about Eddard. For a year he had petulantly ignored the man, and all the while he must have been grieving for the loss of his wife.

"Not grieving," Eddard said at one of their last meetings when Samuel was bold enough to bring it up. "I told you. I forgave her. You grieve things that are lost. She isn't lost. She's taken care of. I love her and knowing she's happy is a good thing."

"Aren't you sad?"

"Of course I am, but love isn't a zero sum game. I took a vow to love and protect her. I only held up one part of that bargain. I think of her but I don't grieve."

"I'm sorry."

"One of these days you're going to learn when to stop sorrying, but it's clearly going to be after I'm in the ground."

On their last meeting, the day before the vagrants would be vagrants no more, they agreed to write each other.

"Though I don't know if I'll have much of interest to tell you. I think I'll be the one living vicariously through you, especially if you manage to talk to that girl again without falling on your ass."

"I'll do what I can. Don't fall off a train."

"I'll do what I can."

The old man and the twelve year old boy embraced for a brief moment, having been on the same farm for more than a year and been friends for three weeks. The next day, Samuel waved the men off with his father and mother, standing on the railway platform. As the train pulled away, a tear formed at the corner of Samuel's eye, and he did not reach to wipe it away, but let it run its course down his cheek. As the smoke billowed from the front of the train and raced its way towards the caboose, Samuel's eyes remained trained on the spot where Eddard Morley had been standing, waving goodbye. He had looked as beautiful as he had the first day in the south wood, sitting among the twisted, rusting rails. In his place, as the train pulled away and the smoke cleared, there across the platform, was Amelia Fribley.

8

It would take a long time for Samuel to get another chance to speak with Amelia Fribley. In fact, it took years. His letters exchanged with Eddard Morley ceased to mention her at all, although it was the stated reason for their correspondence. After a year or so, Samuel ceased to make up excuses and ways to hide his letters from Eddard. He came out with the truth and told his parents that he was corresponding with Eddard Morley. His mother gave his father a queer sort of look, her face hesitating in rictus for a moment before smiling placidly. His father spoke of it as if it were nothing unusual.

"How's he doing these days?"

"Well. Many of the men are still together, although some have moved on or gone home even. They spend a lot of time in San Francisco."

"Lots of rail activity out there," his father said with a curious lack of emotion.

It was as if his parents had entirely forgotten about the year of their existence when an entire troupe of men had lived in their old barn. It was only a casual remembrance, like the time the cow gave birth to a calf when Samuel was five, nothing more than that. It did not occur to Samuel that it was a dark time in the town, and the nation's history, because it was his youth. A man's youth is always his own golden time, even if the pages of history show it to have been the darkest of ages. He would understand in time.

Samuel was fifteen by the time he had another conversation with Amelia Fribley, barely older than she had been at the time of their last conversation. She was now a nearly grown woman of eighteen who had a job in the Millinery in La Rue. Samuel had seen her a few times getting on the bus to go to work. She was always in such fabulous hats these days, no doubt a perk of the job, but Samuel disliked them. They obscured her face, and those wonderfully light eyes he admired so much, almost as if he could see through them. Her plain brown hair was not obscured entirely by her hats, though it had grown less plain, more blonde over the last few years. Samuel had far from forgotten the tongue-lashing she had given him in the old barn at the party for the vagrants, but he couldn't have blamed her for forgetting. He had occasional dabbles in the romantic over his young years, even kissing Angela Farmer on his parents' covered porch when he was twelve. None of it came to anything, and he managed to avoid the high drama that is usually associated with such adolescent tumblings. He could not quite bring himself to be bothered to the point of careless emotion about any of the other girls, though Amelia Fribley hung over him like a cloud.

He wanted to tell her that she had changed him. He had not changed his mind. He still wanted to leave and go somewhere extraordinary, but he had changed how he spoke about it. It wasn't much, but she had taught him, through Eddard's chastisements, that he was a thoroughly privileged young man. He was conscious of his privilege in a way he hadn't been when he had confronted her in the loft. Eddard had hinted he had known how that event was going to go down as soon as he sent him over. "Though

I'd do it again in a heartbeat," he said in one of his letters. There had been moments over the years when he could have spoken to Amelia. It was after all, a relatively small town. They had exchanged pleasantries politely, and passed each other on the street. They had not lived in utter ignorance of each other, but Samuel had simply been unable to muster the courage to break the polite barrier between them. He imagined her as entirely indifferent, as she had not brought up the conversation ever again, no matter what effect it might have had on him, he thought that he was being presumptuous by thinking it had any lasting effect on her memory. Of course, he could have found out if he had only gathered the courage necessary to string the sentences together. There was no rule against it.

He watched as she was courted again and again, and why shouldn't she have been? She was a beautiful girl in a plain town in the middle of America, and it seemed that every young man wanted his chance. Samuel made no move to stop to any of these young men, but they all failed in their own way. Some described her as "haughty" or "not knowing her place" or as just a bitch, but she consistently turned them all down. She was reliably polite, but always told her suitors that she was not interested in dating. She was getting close to *that age*, and there were unpleasant rumors in town about why she was acting this way, and only the kindest rumors suggested it was due to her haughtiness. It pained Samuel to hear these rumors, but he was nobody. He didn't know her, and had only spoken to her for a few moments years earlier. It would have been indecorous for him to express outrage at rumors targeting her. Luckily for Samuel, no courage on his part ended up being necessary in order for him to have another conversation with Amelia Fribley. On a rainy, Friday morning of his fifteenth year, she came right to the front door.

The whole family was gathered in the front room. There was no fire in the grate, as it was a warm, uncomfortable rain, the worst kind. Blynne, as ever clicked her knitting needles together, forever making something for a winter yet to come. Tom Meller was poring over an accounts book, his brow furrowed and the yellow glow of his desk lamp casting his face in an unfortunate light. Samuel was in a chair by himself by the window, alternately watching the rain slide down the pane and reading a few lines of Keats. Del had ordered him Keats, but Samuel could barely stomach it. It was during one of his moments staring out the window that Samuel saw a figure approaching. She had her clothes pulled tight about her, her head down, and an umbrella that was being whipped by the wind. Samuel did not recognize her by this image.

"There's someone coming up the drive," he said. His father got up from his desk, stowed his spectacles in his shirt pocket, and walked deliberately to the door to answer the caller. Samuel's mother reached to turn the radio dial all the way down. A caller on a rainy Friday morning was better than anything on the radio. Samuel could hear his father and the girl conversing. She had stepped inside the door and the sound of raindrops falling from her coat onto the wooden floor of the entryway echoed through the house.

"Well I think Samuel could help," Tom Meller was saying. "I've got more figures to do before the day's out and Samuel's doing nothing but pleasure reading. Lord knows he has enough time to do that."

"You're really too kind. I'll be sure to repay you somehow. I'll bring something over for you real soon."

"We'd be glad to see you again, Amelia but don't you feel obligated. Come right in for a moment and I'll fetch the layabout."

At that moment, Samuel glued his eyes to his book as his father lead Amelia Fribley into the front room. After four years she simply waltzed into his living room as big as life. She stood to the side of Tom Meller, looking very small. Her hair was plastered to her face, the rain darkening it almost to the color it had been four years earlier. Her eyes were as light as ever. If they were the surface of a pond, a fisherman would have no problem seeing right to the bottom. Tom Meller put his hand gently on her shoulder and addressed his son.

"Samuel, I believe you know Amelia Fribley. You aren't quite the same age, but you must have met in passing."

"Certainly."

"Samuel is well thought of," Amelia said.

"Nice to hear," Tom Meller said. "Although a tad surprising," he added good naturedly. "Samuel, Amelia here has missed her bus to La Rue and is going to be late to work if she doesn't get there somehow.

"I'm sorry."

"No need to be sorry, son. You're going to be a part of the solution. I've volunteered you to drive Ms. Fribley to La Rue. You'll take my truck. You know the way. It's straight down the road and straight back. Can't hardly mess it up even if you were reading poetry at the wheel, which you will not be doing. Ms. Fribley will make certain of that."

Samuel thought he saw a blush tinge her face as his father spoke. It was only around young women that his father seemed to let his guard down and be an obliging host. As soon as she was gone, he would return to his usual, solemn self, upset with the numbers and the price of fencing materials and unhappy about the forecast. There was always something. Yet, around Amelia Fribley here was a bright, cheery man. Samuel could not bring himself to look at his mother, for he feared she was either angry or aroused, and he wanted to see neither.

"I can do that. I'll just need to fetch my boots."

Samuel nearly tripped over himself getting up the stairs and getting his boots on. He was shaking. He willed himself to calm. He'd hardly be able to drive if he was shaking so awfully, and she'd be sure to notice. He took three deep breaths and made his way back down the steps. His father was back at his desk, spectacles on his nose, but turned to look at his son.

"We were beginning to worry."

Amelia stood patiently by the coat rack in the entryway, her hands clasped in front of her holding her umbrella. Samuel said goodbye to his parents and vowed to be careful with the truck before grabbing the keys from the bowl by the door. He motioned for Amelia to walk out the door before him, unable yet to form words directed at her, and they were on their way. The truck was around the house, parked by the screen porch. It was unlocked and they each hopped in, Samuel putting the key in the ignition. It didn't turn over immediately, but when it did the engine roared to life confidently, and the gas gauge settled near the F. Tom Meller ran a tight ship, and it extended to every aspect of his farm. It was at times like these that Samuel felt a genuine admiration for his father. It of course further cemented his surety that he could never be like his father, but there was a certain begrudging admiration that came out from time to time. He put the car in drive and headed for the country road directly West of the Meller farm.

"Thank you again," Amelia said quietly. "I'd lose my job if it weren't for you. I can't believe I missed the bus."

"It happens."

"Have you ever taken the bus?"

"Well, no."

"I'm sorry, I didn't mean to...well thank you."

They were silent for a time, the only sound the hum of the engine, the rolling of the tires over the wet concrete, and the wipers' continual squeaking as they kept Samuel's line of vision clear. It was a full thirty minutes to La Rue, and there was an ineffable boundary between them. It might have been the bad conditions, the necessity of his looking forward and remaining bodily occupied on something else, but Samuel was able, now in a situation to do so finally, to bring up the last time they had spoken.

"Do you remember it?"

"I do," she said. "Quite well. You had a lot to say. You were a very opinionated young man. What were you, eleven?"

"Ten. I'm fifteen now, but you're right. I'm sure I was a real jerk."

"No," she said. "Well, yes. But no. You weren't exactly eloquent about it, but you convinced me of something that day and I've not forgotten. You convinced me to leave this place, and I've set my sights on it ever since. I'd never given it any serious thought before, and here you came, this kid younger than me with absolute certainty that he was leaving. It left me feeling like I wasn't thinking big enough."

Samuel hardly knew how to react to the news that she too remembered that conversation from the old barn. Amelia didn't just remember it, she too had thought of it often in the years since, and here they had been passing each other in silence when they could have been speaking the whole time.

At that moment, Samuel was forced to slam on the brakes to avoid another truck pulling slowly into the road from a country lane. The Meller truck came to a skidding halt as the other truck slowly accelerated and pulled away. Both Amelia and Samuel were breathing audibly.

"Sorry," Samuel said. "It came out of nowhere."

"Must be why you keep your face so close to those books."

"Pardon?"

"Just that I saw it coming pretty easily. Have you had your eyes checked?"

"My eyes are fine."

"Suit yourself."
Samuel's unnecessary defense of his eyes lead to a stall in the conversation and he was angry at himself for it. Why couldn't he just let it go? Now how could he find the strength to bring up that he'd so often thought of that conversation they'd had in the barn, and how he wished he had spoken differently, more sensibly. There was nothing for it now. He had ruined his moment. They drove in silence. There were no more near-death accidents and before he knew it, Samuel was idling in front of the Frobisher's Fine Millinery storefront in La Rue.

"Do I need to wait for you?"

"I can catch the bus home. I won't miss that one. I can't thank you enough. I meant what I said to your father. I'll be sure to bring something by soon."

Samuel smiled and nodded, unsure what else the protocol was in such a situation. She smiled back and closed the truck door].It was not until he was nearly halfway back down the county road that Samuel realized she had left her umbrella behind. He was filled with a renewed sense of possibility. He had spent the last several years without an excuse to begin a conversation with Amelia Fribley, and now he was given two in the same day. He had shared a car ride with her, and now he had something of hers that surely needed to be returned. It would be rude to keep it, but gentlemanly to return it. For a moment, Samuel even allowed himself to imagine that she had left the umbrella on purpose. Maybe she had intended for Samuel to try to speak to her again. It was certainly possible wasn't it? Anything seemed possible on that rainy morning. He had been thrust into companionship with Amelia, and had even learned that she too had given much thought to and been changed by the conversation they had years before. Anything was possible indeed. And to think, only a short hour earlier, Samuel had been reading a particularly boring series of poems by a poet that he found laborious at best.

Back at the farmhouse, it was almost as if nothing spectacular had happened at all. His mother remained knitting, and her father was still bent over his books. It could have been only the blink of an eye past when Amelia knocked on the door. An absurd, fleeting thought told

Samuel that it had all been a fever dream, but his father's voice interrupted his roiling mind.

"Put the truck back where it belongs?"

"Yes, sir."

"Everything go alright?"

"Does Doctor Milliband check eyes?"

Two days later, holding a slip from Doctor Milliband with inscrutable numbers on it, Samuel stood outside of Del's wondering if the books had ruined his eyes, if reading in the dim, filtered light of the south wood were what made his vision just so bad.

"Surprised you can get your fork to your mouth to be honest," the kindly doctor had said, chuckling to himself. "But our bodies are miraculous things. Something you learn when you deal with them as much as I do. We always find ways to adjust, and I imagine your body's natural rhythms have attuned themselves to your vision. It might be strange initially when you get your spectacles, and might even have some dizziness, but you'll soon appreciate seeing the world for all it is."

Samuel was to give Del the piece of paper along with the address of a lens maker in Chicago. In four to six weeks, Samuel was to have a pair of his very own spectacles that he was intended to wear all the time. Unlike Tom Meller, who wore them only to do figures, Samuel was meant to always be bespectacled. At first, it was a blow to the young man's ego, and he was certainly still worried about his appearance, but he was able to settle his nerves by telling himself how it separated father from son, farmer from budding academic.

9

Despite his obvious motivating factors, Samuel failed to bring Amelia her umbrella for a full eight days. On the ninth day, she appeared again at the door bearing the promised present. It was near dusk, and she held a pie in her hands, covered in a cloth.

"What do we have here?" Tom Meller said.

"It's cherry. For all your trouble the other week."

"Do come in, Amelia. Let's cut you a slice."

"That's really not necessary."

"But I insist."

Amelia was learning that Tom Meller was forceful in everything he did, even his courtesy. Samuel sat stiffly across the table from her while the Meller family and their guest all made a great show of enjoying the pie.

"Delicious, dear," Blynne said politely putting her fork down after only a few bites.

"Excellent timing," Tom said. "We'd only finished dinner moments before you arrived. A better dessert could not have been asked for."

Amelia looked up at Samuel as if it was his turn to speak. Every other Meller had spoken in turn about the pie, but Samuel ate his in relative silence. He managed a smile and a noncommittal agreement with his parents' assessment of the pie. It was a painfully awkward moment for the youth, and he could not help but with that all of the plans he and Eddard Morley had hatched were closer to his mind. They were four years old and quickly eroding from his memory in all but the most hazy terms. It had always seemed over the last four years that at least he was prepared if the opportunity presented itself. He and Eddard had covered those bases, and if he was ever to receive the opportunity to speak to her again, he would know what to do. And yet when the moment came, he found himself utterly without words.

Amelia was already out the door and walking down the drive before Samuel was able to kick himself into gear. His parents watched in confusion as he bolted out the door, holding an unfamiliar umbrella and raced towards the young girl from down the road.

"You forgot," Samuel said panting. "Your umbrella. The other day I mean. In the car. In case you need it again."

"Thank you. That's very kind of you."
She took the proffered umbrella and stood with it held over her stomach expectantly.

"I got glasses."

"What?"

"You were right. I needed glasses. Doctor Milliband said it was lucky I could get food to my mouth." What a stupid thing to say, and there it was, unable to be taken back, forever a part of their conversation.

"I didn't mean anything by it. I wasn't trying to be cruel. I think it's wonderful how much you read. It's a good thing."

"I want to go to Ohio State and study literature."

"That's a wonderful plan. Make sure you do. That way, if there's a war in Europe, you'll be last on the list of those to go."

"My father says there won't be any war."

"Well what do you think?"

"If there is, I'll go."

"That's a rather stupid thing to say."

"I don't think so. If there's a war, it'll be much more important than school."

"Is that what your father thinks?"

"That's what I think."

"Well let's hope there isn't any war then," she said, turning to go. "Thank you for my umbrella."

Samuel remained outside as she made her way down the long, Meller drive and back onto the county road. How was it that every conversation they had ended so poorly? It seemed that they could not speak to each other for any length of time without one of them getting upset at the other. Still, she had shown a concern for his well being that was encouraging. If she didn't want him to go to war, then maybe she wanted him to stick around. That had to count for something. When Samuel got back inside, his parents were discussing something with great concentration.

"Samuel, did you see the hat Amelia was wearing?" His mother asked.

"Yes. I suppose I did. She makes hats."

"It was a cloche. I thought it was darling."

"It was a hat," Tom Meller said.

"Your father doesn't think I need a cloche hat, though I think it would look very nice for church and going into town."

"What use does a farm wife have for a bell looking hat?"

"For your information Thomas, I am not only your wife. I exist independently of you, no matter what your books say. Farm wife or not, I think it was a lovely hat."

"I can find out what they cost for you," Samuel said slowly. "If you want."

"What harm can that do?" Blynne said. "But be polite, do. Don't make a big fuss of it. It's not nice to talk about money so publicly. Make it clear that it's because I thought it looked so darling on her."

"Yes mother."

Tom Meller grunted and opened the back door, muttering to himself as he went.

Once again, Samuel was gifted with an opportunity to interact with Amelia, and he was determined to make this one count. Fribley was no last name for an Amelia, he thought. Certainly not. He could not very well take the truck down to the millinery in La Rue, so Samuel would have to simply waltz up to the Fribley house and ask to see her. To Samuel's great disappointment, when he did so three days later, it was her father who answered the door.

"'Melia's taking dinner with the Cartwrights this evening. She's good friends with that Sheila. You want to buy one of those fancy head toppers she spends all her time drawing?"

"Not me sir, but my mother was quite taken with the cloche she was wearing the other day."

"Cloak?"

"Cloche, sir. It's shaped like a bell."

It was a great pain for Samuel to call Mr. Fribley "sir," but he had prepared himself with absolute certainty not to get into an argument with Amelia this time and was equipped with an abundance of superficial patience for this particular encounter.

"Look funny to me," he said, as if there was nothing else to be done about it.

"Can't account for taste. Either way it lies, my mother would-"

"I'll send her by the house," Fribley said, cutting Samuel off. "She's got a dis-play she brings around to try and sell to lady magazines. I'll let her know. You've got my word."

There was nothing else to be done. Again, Samuel would have to wait to receive Amelia at his parents' home. Mr. Fribley had made it abundantly clear that Samuel would not be welcome to sit and wait for his daughter's return, and that he did not fancy exchanging words with Samuel in the first place. He was really a most unpleasant man to Samuel, and it was almost impossible to believe that Amelia was his daughter. He was inclined to think more favorably of the situation when he thought of how different he was from his own father.

Samuel thanked Amelia's father and made his way back home down the country road with his hands buried deep in his pockets. Despite the incredible amount of words he had exchanged with Amelia over the last few weeks, especially in comparison to the number of zero for the four previous years, it was hard not to be disappointed at being greeted only by her father. Samuel had quickly become greedy for time spent in her presence, despite the fact that he often felt frustrated or outmatched every time she left him. She was older and wiser than him and it showed at every opportunity. He was just then beginning to realize that a woman with Amelia's qualities of independence, surety, and grace were not only the building blocks of profound frustration, but also of an abiding respect and love. The side of the coin resting opposite of frustration was still just a feeling, a hunger to be in her presence, but it was blossoming all the same. He waited impatiently for her to call on his mother.

Days passed and there was no sign of Amelia dropping by. The Fribleys did not have a telephone, so there was nothing to do but be patient. Blynne seemed perfectly willing to wait as long as necessary, and was not nearly as upset by the delay as her son.

"She's a busy, young working woman," she said offhandedly. "I'm sure she'll fit me in whenever she can." There was something about the way Samuel's mother spoke of Amelia. It almost seemed like Blynne was a little bit jealous of the autonomy that the young woman displayed for the whole world to see. Although he had been preoccupied by his own concerns, it struck Samuel as unusual, his mother's sudden interest in hats and her assertion that she was not simply Tom's wife. Samuel spent the intervening days much as he always had the last several years of his life. He took generously long walks in the south wood, but held off on bringing books with him. His relationship with literature was at a rocky point, as he now blamed books for ruining his vision. Besides, he did not figure on being able to focus very much on the romantic musings of others while his own were so much on his mind. Instead, his walks were mostly composed of his personal rambles, both in his mind and by his feet. He often found himself in corners of the woods he had not traversed in years. Though he knew the woods almost step by step in their entirety, he generally did not stray far from the paths he had worn through the trees in his years as a wanderer of the Meller property. It consistently amazed Samuel that there were not already well-worn tracks in the wood when he was a child. He was not the first Meller to grow up on the property, but for some reason Tom Meller had never much explored the south woods, except to retrieve firewood or to practice shooting at targets.

"Explored?" Samuel's father once said in response to his son. "What's to explore? It's all about the same. Elder trees mostly. All hundred acres are close to the same. I've been down to the fence a few times to check up on it, though I don't see how a few people wandering through minding their own business makes much difference."

Samuel had been unable to continue that conversation with his father, as the two men were so far apart in thinking that it scarcely made sense to attempt a dialogue.

Samuel could not fathom how his father could see the south woods as a monolithic entity. Samuel knew intimately the subtle differences between places mere meters apart. Tom Meller was technically correct that it was mostly alder trees, though the old man could not pronounce the species correctly, but there was so much more. There were Ash trees, their bark cut through like so many wrinkles, their branches spread out over wide swaths, providing excellent shade that was always sure to include the chattering of any number of squirrels that loved to nest in their ample branches. There were aspen, shockingly white in appearance with spots like dalmatian dogs and leaves an unfathomably, bumblebee yellow in the fall time that covered the ground and outshone all of the other leaves and needles on the forest floor. There were cranberry bushes, some that were entirely globular and looked as if they would begin to roll away to another part of the forest if the wind picked up too much. Samuel treated each with a special reverence, touching each with his hand as he walked by, sometimes stopping to take notice of a subtle change. He had been greatly affected by

Thoreau's assertion that man learns the most about himself when he is watching the small changes in nature about him. It was always a fresh and present surprise to Samuel when he noticed a small change in the south wood, a constant reminder that it was an ever-changing organism that he wandered in and out of from time to time.

Samuel used these walks to center himself, to place his body exactly where it needed to be so that he could once again understand his own insignificance in the world. Unlike his heroes of the literary canon, Samuel did not imagine his insignificance as a calming, reassuring piece of information. It is hardly a crime to misread at a young age, and what Samuel saw in his walks, no matter how much he loved them, was his own life put into a stark, unflattering context. Samuel deeply wanted to matter, to make change, and to be remembered. His love for nature was partially one of intense jealousy, and of continued frustration. He felt insignificant, and his inability to simply bear his soul to Amelia and be done with it only exacerbated his adolescent pain. It did not make sense. Why did it have to be such a game? He wanted to stand in front of her and show her all that he loved and in turn she could show him all that she loved. He wanted her to understand him more than anything, to understand his intense desire to prove himself more than a farmer. But it was not possible to bare one's soul in a single moment of exposure, no matter how much he wished it were. He did not think Amelia was compelled to love him back, or to think that anything he valued was worthwhile. Samuel simply wanted to be able to communicate everything in his heart and mind to her so that she could have it and do with it what she would.

When Amelia did show up to show Blynne her selection of hats, Samuel was little more than a spectator. On the day in question, Amelia strolled up their driveway confidently, a suitcase with two, large steel buckles on the side under her arm, and her head curiously sans hat. She knocked primly, politely, and smiled broadly when Blynne answered the door. When Amelia had been spotted coming up the drive, Tom Meller suddenly remembered some equipment that needed checking in the barn. For his part, Samuel sat in the rocking chair while his mother and Amelia sat on the couch, the suitcase open in front of them.

"My, I don't know where to begin. I only asked you over because I was such an admirer of your cloche from the other day."

"That old thing? That was one of the first hats I made. The stitching's all uneven. That's why I wear it myself. I couldn't afford a good one. The materials aren't my own you see."

"Oh," Blynne said, shocked at her own inability to judge hat workmanship.

"Not to worry. I'm sure we'll find one equally suitable for you in my little collection here. Now, I want you to know that I can make you one special. If there are aspects of these you don't like, we can always go the custom route."

"I don't know about all that. Tom-"

"Oh don't you worry about that," Amelia said, winking at the woman old enough to be her mother. "This is on me. I'll make it on my own time. We'll split the cost of the materials and the labor I'll be happy to do."

"I can't possibly-"

"Of course you can. And your husband will be happier as well. All I ask is that when your friends ask where you got it...you tell them. Nothing more."

"I'm certain I can manage that."

"Let's get to work then."

Samuel was amazed at the way the young woman dealt with his mother in conversation. Was she really only three years his senior? It seemed nearly a lifetime. He could understand deeply complicated sentiments from his books (or so he imagined he could), but there was no way he could have struck a deal like that so effortlessly. His conversation on Mr. Fribley's front steps came back to him as an unflattering parallel with Amelia's chatter with Blynne. His mind wandered as his eyes lost focus on the pages folded in his lap.

"Well," Amelia was saying. "I agree that it's the loveliest hat of the bunch, but I'm afraid I couldn't recreate it if I wanted to. We don't know the next time we'll get a shipment in and they are quite expensive."

"What a shame."

Samuel looked over and saw his mother poring over a hat with a great deal of feathers and leaves festooned about it.

"What is it that's so expensive about a hat like that?" he said.

Amelia smiled at him as one might to a small child asking about the color of the sky.

"The feathers of course. The peacock especially."

"Why would you pay for a thing like that?"

"I believe the economists call it scarcity."

There was her cutting wit again. Remembering their past conversations, Samuel renegotiated in his mind before responding.

"Why they aren't scarce at all. I could have a bundle in no time."

"How is that?"

"The south wood is full of feathers. I collected them as a kid. I can show you if you'd like. Probably still got some in my bedroom. Guinea hen, red tail hawk, peacock, Canadian goose, you name it I've got it. No one's hunted on our property except our family in a century and birds aren't stupid. They stop in alright. Time to time I'll be walking underneath a tree and it'll just...erupt. Quite a sight."

"I'd very much like to see this collection. If you don't mind."

"Just a moment."

Samuel was as surprised by the turn of events as Amelia was. He never would have thought that bird feathers were of so much use to anyone. He'd stopped collecting them years ago; he hadn't seen the point any longer. It was a child's activity. He brought back down an old cigar box. As promised, it had just about every type of feather he'd mentioned.

"You can have those if you like. Most are a bit crumpled from the box."

"And you can get more?"

Amelia had dropped any pretense of paying attention to Blynne. Her eyes were locked with Samuel, an intensity behind their translucent edges which he had never seen before.

"Of course."

"Would you be willing to show me this?"

"Don't see why not."

She took him by surprise. She lunged forward, very nearly knocking her suitcase display over in the process, and enveloped Samuel in an unthinking hug. It was the first time they had ever physically touched, and every cell in Samuel's body was afire. Amelia separated herself from him quickly, realizing her indiscretion.

"Excuse me, Mrs. Meller."

"It's quite alright to be excited," Blynne said. "Does this mean my hat is back on the menu?"

"It does. It certainly does."

10

The following afternoon was settled on as when Samuel would take Amelia into the south wood to show her where he could find feathers to be used in her hats. She smiled politely at Samuel as she left that night, blushing a little, perhaps remembering their hug, promising to be on time the next day. Samuel could not help but think of how so long ago, Eddard Morley had told him to show her what he loved. And now he could. He was going to have that opportunity. That night, Samuel wrote his first letter to Eddard in many months. He hoped that he was still working for the railroad and that his letter would find its way to the old man somehow. Eddard deserved to know that all of their planning had not come to nothing after all.

She was prompt the following afternoon, just as she said she would be, and was dressed for the occasion. She wore long pants, hiked high above her waist and belted with a man's, well-worn brown belt, the loose end tucked under. She wore a paint-stained shirt tucked in neatly, and a pair of work boots. Her hair was pulled into a bun, and she was hat-less once more. Samuel could not help but chuckle. He was taking her into the south wood, and she had prepared herself for the Amazon.

"You look ready," he said.

"Yes. I've brought a satchel to pick up anything interesting as well."

Her earnest nature was nearly as endearing as her apparent belief that the south wood of the Meller property was a place that required such strenuous preparation.

"Well let's get going then."

He lead her along some of his favorite paths, pointing out spots that were particularly beautiful or noteworthy. He showed her the white ash in which he had painstakingly carved a Whitman verse, the dirt and grime of years causing his juvenile etchings to stand out a dark black against the white trunk.

"That there," Samuel said, pointing to a cranberry bush that reached to his shoulder. "Was no more than a foot high a few years ago, and there was this bird, a wren, that was absolutely determined to make a nest in the top.

Of course, the bush wasn't strong enough to hold much up, and every time I'd walk by here, the wren would be working hard to put the nest back together, only to have it fall down again. Birds are like people that way, I guess."

"What happened to the bird, do you know?"

"Sure I do."

Samuel lead her up to the globular bush and pointed inside. In the middle of the bush, at an intersection of several interior branches, was an old bird nest.

"She figured it out."

"So she did."

Amelia smiled widely at this as they continued on their walk in the woods, more amazed at Samuel's casual nature in the woods than at the facts of the wren's nest. He was almost a different person under the cover of trees.

"You really love it here, don't you?"

"It's my favorite part of the property. Never really felt like part of the farm. The rows of corn, the cows, the barns, they all seem so far away from this. They seem like an aberration, an unnatural way for land to look that's become useful to us for food but is so much uglier and less pleasant. The south wood has always been my home. I started walking here when I was little more than a baby."

"It really is lovely. What's that tree there called?"

"That? Why that's just a black alder. My father says that's all the south wood is… some alders that lead to the fence line of our property."

"Well anyone can see that's not true."

"He can't."

They walked in silence for a long time, Amelia appreciating Samuel's most intimate of spaces, although it was an open-air space, it felt as if she were in his bedroom, peeking through his drawers, or reading his diary if he kept one. This place was personal to him, and his knowledge of the place bore it out.

"Where do you usually find feathers?"

"All over. Varies. But I'm taking you to where I've probably found the most. We're just taking the scenic route. Generally though, your best shot is near water. Like any other creatures, birds need water. You're most likely to find more nests in trees, bushes, and holes that are close to a water source. There's a stream a ways back we're headed to."

"What's it called?"

"It doesn't appear on any map or anything. It's not big enough to warrant it, but I've taken to calling it Morley's Creek."

"Why's that?"

"I figure that things should be named after good people. Too often that's not the case. Just whoever finds it. What kind of an accomplishment is that, finding a thing? So it's not Samuel's creek, or Meller's creek, but Morley's."

"Who's Morley?"

"A good man."

Amelia did not pressure him to explain himself further, but she did note that it was the first time he had seemed to be holding back since they had crossed the treeline from the fields into the wood. As they neared the creek, Samuel told Amelia to watch the shape of the trees.

"Why?"

"I think you'll figure it out on your own."

As they walked, Samuel tried not to stare as she made an exaggerated show of looking around her, her head on a swivel. Birds chirped and a light breeze shook the leaves of the canopy gently. When they stood on the banks of the creek, the sounds of the water gently flowing over smooth stones, she turned to him.

"They lean."

"They do. The closer you get to the creek, the more noticeable it is. They shape themselves towards the water. Eventually, it's like it is here. The creek becomes a green tunnel as the trees on both sides reach over in their greediness."

"It really is beautiful."

"Once, a few years ago, I laid on my back and floated downstream looking up so that I could see what it was like."

"And?"

"It was terrifying. I felt powerless and claustrophobic. I've never done it again."

"Is that your greatest fear? Powerlessness?"

"Probably."

"Not mine. Mine's more simple than that. My greatest fear is pain. Powerlessness could go either way. You could be powerless and perfectly fine, or you could be in agony. I fear the agony, whether I'm in control or not."

"I suppose we'll both have to just be afraid then."

"We'll live with it I think," Amelia said. "Now didn't we come out here to find some feathers?"
Samuel lead her along the creek, following it with ease. He had long ago worked paths into the undergrowth along the creek, and the two of them followed them while keeping their eyes peeled. It was Amelia who spotted one first, a small one, but beautiful.

"Looks like a crow to me," Samuel said. "Bad omen."

"I think it's wonderful. She placed it gently in her satchel."

"Suit yourself."
A little further on, it was Samuel who found a perfectly white feather.

"Duck," he said. "Mallard."

"I thought Mallards were the green and black ones?"

"You've got it right. They have some white in their wings. That's where this is from."

Over the course of an hour or so, they found dozens of feathers. They stopped to take a break, took their shoes off and dipped their toes in the creek. It was pleasingly cool, and they each sat pleasantly watching the water break over their feet. Amelia gently upended her satchel and piled up her feathers on a bed of moss.

"Quite a haul you've got there," Samuel said.

"Yes. Yes it is."

Amelia took the crow feather and twirled it between her thumb and forefinger. Her eyes watched it with closeness before she flicked it into the creek and watched it begin to float away.

"I thought you liked that one?"

"I did."

Next, she took a bluish, gray feather that neither of them had been able to identify. That too, she flicked into the creek and watched wordlessly as it floated away. This she repeated until there were only three feathers left.

"These will do," she said, standing up and reaching for her socks on the bank.

"What was wrong with the others?"

"Nothing," she said. "Didn't you say there was an abundance of feathers in the wood?"

"Well sure."

"I suppose I'll have to come back then."

11

Amelia appeared once more at the Meller residence, this time with bolts of cloth in tow. Tom Meller answered the door and let out a deep breath.

"You're starting to become a regular fixture around here."

"I hope you don't think I'm intruding."

"Course not, Amelia. Come in. What did you think of the South Wood? Is it as majestic as my son seems to think? Spends most of his life there."

"It's lovely, and importantly there are an abundance of feathers."

"Never much took to hunting, 'cept to break the boredom, so there's plenty of birds. They know where to go."

"That's what Samuel said."

"Well he's learned something of use from his books then. Come on, Blynne's shelling peas. I'll let her know you're here."

There was a great deal of indecision about the fabric for Blynne's hat. The woman in her middle age approached the task as if it was the only decision she had made in her entire life. Eventually, they decided on a lovely, maroon color that would be offset by some startling white feathers.

"Your son helped me find them."

"Who knew he could be so useful?"

The two women laughed and Blynne put her hand on Amelia's knee gently, her mouth open, but forming no words, a fit of girlish giggles overcoming her.

"Is he here?" Amelia said. "Samuel?"

"No, he's in town. Had a delivery come sooner than expected."

"A delivery?"

"His spectacles."

"How nice."

"I'd not bring it up. He's none too excited about it. He's more sensitive to looking bookish than he lets on."

"I'm sure it will be fine. I only hoped to gather some more feathers. I'll just have to wait until next time."

"You've not learned where they are for yourself? I'm sure Mr. Meller would have no objection to you retrieving them."

"No, I'm afraid I'm hopeless when it comes to the outdoors. I'd get lost in a heartbeat. Really, it's no worry. I can wait."

The trips into the south wood did continue after a few days time, and Amelia was careful not to mention Samuel's new spectacles unless he brought it up. She did not want to hurt his feelings. She was surprised to find he was wearing them even as they walked through the wood. She had imagined him leaving them only for reading, and keeping them neatly tucked into his shirt pocket until needed. However, this was not the case. The truth was that Samuel could not bring himself to take them off. The wood that he loved so dearly had become an entirely new, and even more wonderful place. It was drawn in such sharper detail, he could hardly believe it. It was enough to make the spectacles worth it. It seemed miraculous that he had fallen in love with the wood in the first place with only being able to see the bastardization his eyes had allowed. The black ants crawling up the trunk of a white ash stuck out as clearly as the full moon against a midnight sky.

"I feel as if I have to read again all of the texts I've ever read about man's relationship to nature."
"Why?"
"I can't imagine I understood them correctly without having seen what it actually looks like."
Amelia laughed gently, the sound of her laughs being drowned out by a breeze that shook the leaves over their heads.
"I'm sure you understood them just fine. Words can't do all this justice anyway. It's just a man's best effort is all."
"I'd not thought of it that way."
"Have you written about this place?"
"I've tried."
"And?"
"Not gotten so far."

"So perhaps Walden is nothing quite like you think. Maybe our friend Henry couldn't truly do it justice on paper. It could very well be impossible."

"You've read Walden?"

"Certainly, though most of it is terribly dull. I liked the chapter on visitors. That one was lively enough."

It was Samuel's turn to laugh. It was fair to bemoan Thoreau for his lack of flair or charisma. Still, he was a kindred spirit.

"We've not found any feathers yet," Samuel said.

"Is that a problem?"

"Not to my mind. I thought it might be to you."

"And here I thought you were seeing so clearly."

"I am."

"Are you? Or will you continue to pretend you are unaware of what I mean."

"It's difficult."

"More difficult than keeping your feelings under wraps and dancing around them all day long while we look for feathers?"

"Perhaps."

"Do you love me?"

Amelia stopped walking. Samuel walked a few steps more before he realized she had stopped. Her arms were crossed over her chest. She wore a shawl, her men's pants and boots once more, and a look of sheer determination on her face. Her feet were set, one caddy corner to the other, a position taking by a woman who was not about to accept silence as an answer. Amelia was prepared to wait as long as was necessary for her answer.

"There's a bird's nest above your right shoulder," Samuel said, taking a step towards her.
Amelia remained where she was. Samuel walked until he was face to face with Amelia, and reached into the empty bird's nest while still locking his eyes on her. He pulled out a handful of detritus, and from it, plucked three white, downy feathers. He gently opened the satchel at her side and let them fall in.

"I always have," he said. "I loved you the moment I first spoke to you and you tore me to shreds. I loved you for four years after that, and every day since you've come back into my life. You are smarter, more confident, and generally a more worthy human being than I am, and you frustrate the hell out of me. From the first moment we've met, you've challenged me, and I can't think of a better definition of love than that. When I was nine years old, I spent three weeks in this wood with an old man whose wife left him, who wanted to plant the seeds of a younger, more successful generation of love, planning out what I'd say to you if I ever got the chance to speak with you again. When the time came, I'd forgotten every word that was spoken on the subject. In fact, I didn't know what to say. I've never been very good at speaking off the cuff. I either remain silent or reel off a book-length speech like this because I think I'm better on paper. Most no one likes to listen to me when I get going like this, so I figure I ought to stop. To answer your question again: of course I do. I don't doubt that I always will. That's about the shape of it."

Amelia wrapped her hands behind Samuel's neck and pulled him down to her. She parted her lips slightly and kissed the boy from the old barn.

12

Their love was as swift in blossoming as it was slow in forming. Samuel and Amelia each felt an obligation to cram as much love and emotion into each moment they shared together to make up for the four years they could have had. In an instant, they were discussing their future lives together, walking hand in hand in the south wood, still nominally collecting feathers for Amelia's hat-making. The hat for Blynne was nearly finished, and Mrs. Meller was delighted with the progress. In reality, the two lovers spent most of their time mapping their lives out, and very little time looking for feathers. There were many agreements. On kids, they both fancied two the proper number, and each wanted to live in a small house. Their disagreements they brushed aside like so many young couples, unable to imagine that they would ever truly come between them. Samuel stubbornly believed he must leave their town in order to find success, while Amelia wanted to stay. She promised not to come between him and his studies, telling him with all the passion of a young heart that it would be her heart's joy and duty to wait for him to return from university.

"I'll wait for you," she said, again and again. Their disagreement that seemed most pressing at the time was about how to tell their parents.

"Why should we do that?" Samuel said. "Then they will stifle us at every turn, make it impossible for us to see each other, spend time alone together until we're married."

"But it's the right thing to do. We must tell them. I can't stay in town waiting for you without them knowing. It would eat me up inside."

"You mean, you want a public declaration as a buffer against my skipping town, is that it?"

"Of course not. I don't imagine you'd abandon me. I simply can't abide by lying to my parents, or yours."

"Let's run away. Marry me. Move with me when I'm in university. Then we will come back and already be married. No one will be able to keep us apart then."

"Absolutely not. I'll not be talked of as a Trollope by running away as if we're ashamed. It is simple. We tell them. It's not a crime, and I'll not be ashamed. Now, the manner of telling your own parents I'll leave up to you, but I insist our love be public knowledge before you run off to school."

"Very well," Samuel said, staring at his shoes and the soft indentations they were making in the mud.

"Come now," Amelia said. "Don't be cross. Look up at me."

He did, and she pecked him on the lips and stood back from him, smiling broadly, too much for Samuel to remain angry at, and he cracked a smile of his own.

"There he is," she said. "My Samuel."

The town got used to seeing the two young people together, and even began to like to see the handsome couple walking down the road hand in hand, or waiting at the bus stop together for the bus that would take her to the millinery. It was often noted that the Meller boy would stay at the bus stop long after the bus had taken Amelia away, his line of vision still aimed at where the bus had been. He would sit with his hands resting gently on his knees, looking out at where his love had been. Only after minutes of silence would he pat his knees and get up. What would happen when the Meller boy went off to school? It was sure to happen. He was very bright. Everyone knew that. Would she wait for him? Would they be married before he left so that she could accompany him? In a town with little to talk about, a young couple was a gift from the gossip gods.

The Meller folks seemed happy enough with the match. The Fribley girl was poor, sure, but anyone could see she was of a more noble stock than her father.

"Fribley's no name for such a girl," folks could be heard whispering outside Del's store, and that was the common belief.

The Meller's were not a prejudiced family, and made no mention of Amelia's lack of wealth, but were only ever heard saying nice things about the girl. Blynne was often seen wearing the hats the girl made at the millinery, and there was a rumor that even Tom Meller had a new working hat and wouldn't say where he'd gotten it from.

The young couple became a nice distraction for folks that didn't want to talk about the coming war in Europe. Much had changed from 1937 to 1938. It seemed more likely than ever that there was going to be war, with Hitler seemingly unable to be satisfied with whatever the international community was willing to give him. He wanted it all. Even the men of middle Ohio recognized it in the diminutive German's face.

"That's a look that needs no language," Del said to his friend, Tom Meller. "And needs no spurring on neither."

"I know it," Tom said, sighing deeply.
Tom Meller had long thought that a war was imminent, but had put on a face that indicated otherwise. His son had been asking him for a few years if there was going to be a war, but Tom could not bring himself to tell Samuel what struck him as the obvious truth. There was something in Samuel, something glory-seeking, and so foreign to his father, that the man feared speaking the truth aloud. He feared for his son and what he might do. The sudden appearance of Amelia in his son's life had helped Tom to

sleep at night. Amelia was smart, grounded, and a logical sort of girl. She was a damn sight better than her father, and would do well to settle Samuel as well. Tom imagined that if his son really loved the girl, and it seemed obvious to all that he did, then his fool son wouldn't be able to rush into death quite so quickly. Samuel would have to think about Amelia if a war was on. He would have to think of her first. Tom would never tell his son to shirk his duty if the call came down, but he knew his son, and Samuel had the look of a volunteer about him. Amelia could help with that sort of reckless behavior, reign him in. Tom had even witnessed it. The two of them had been reading aloud together from a book of poetry near his fireplace recently, and it had pleased Tom.

"That makes no sense at all," Amelia said. "There's no such thing as mermaids."

"That's not the point," Samuel said. "It's about a feeling. He's afraid of dying. The voices that wake him are human. He *grows old*."

"Why not just say that then? Why bring up mermaids at all?"

"I think you're focusing on the wrong aspect."

"If it's wrong to focus on it, then I suppose it shouldn't have been included in the first place. Haven't I heard you say that before?"

"Well...yes."

"So Eliot should have revised again, shouldn't he have?"

"I suppose so."

Tom watched out of the corner of his eye as his son closed the book of poetry on his lap and took Amelia's hand in his own, his thumb making concentric circles in her palm. Tom had never seen his son accept defeat in a matter of academics or poetry like that before. Any number of times he or his wife had offered some gentle rebuke about a poem he had read proudly aloud, and he had spent long hours telling them just why they were wrong, and yet here was this girl, uneducated but bright as Samuel for certain, and he accepted her judgment right away. He deferred to her in a way that was comforting to Tom Meller. He believed that his son had finally been tamed, that the spirit in Samuel that had always frightened him, had finally reached a more logical resting place. Tom thought that perhaps it had never been his job to temper his son's spirit. It had always been a job for Amelia to accomplish, or she wouldn't have captured Samuel's heart as she had. Tom looked on their relationship gladly, and said to Blynne one night,

"She gives me hope, that girl."

"She's a nice, young woman. Has a head on her shoulders, that's for sure."

"More than our son, that's for sure."

"You would think so."

"What is that supposed to mean?"

"It's not supposed to mean anything. You've never seen eye to eye with Samuel. You're entirely different creatures. It hard to believe he is of your body at times. Amelia is like the son you've never had."

"That's absurd."

"Is it? She's industrious, bright, has an appreciation for tradition that Samuel has never had, and which you treasure."

> "I just think she's good for our son."
> "I hope so too, dear. I hope so too."

Samuel Meller's eighteenth birthday was on September first, 1939. A grand party was to be held in the old barn on the Meller property. Days were spent in preparation, sweeping out the old place and bringing in tables and chairs enough for the whole town. It was the first event to take place in the old barn for a long time, though plenty of folks still remembered the party that had been thrown there nearly ten years earlier. It was partially due to those hazy memories that the town was abuzz with excitement and rumor about what kind of expense Tom Meller was going to in order to throw such an elaborate celebration for his son. There were other reasons folks were nervy too. There were rumors flying that Hitler's troops were on the move, and nearly equally abundant rumors that young Samuel was going to take the opportunity of his eighteenth birthday to propose marriage to Amelia Fribley. They had been an item for two years, seemingly becoming only closer over the passage of those years, spending all of their spare moments together, wandering the south wood on the Meller property, reading out loud to each other, their hands intertwined more often than not. It was as if their bodies needed to be touching at all times, or they would simply fall apart into insecure, unglued pieces. They held each other together in some ineffable, but crucial way.

"I'd always thought of the boy as a bit loopy, but she knows what's what."

"He's too good for her. She ought to cut her losses and go back to her father's shack. Know her place."

"I've heard she's already with child."

"Twins, I think."

"He's going to enlist in the army to fight Hitler."

"We aren't going to war. That's Europe's problem. I'm with Lindbergh and his folks."

"Meller's ain't got enough backbone to fight in any wars. They're nothing but land thieves masquerading as well to-do folks. Nothing better than sharecroppers who found a lump of gold in cow shit."

"I heard the party is to have fireworks. A huge display coming in all the way from Alabama."

"Alabama?"

"That's where all the good fireworks are, dummy. Everyone knows that."

"Hitler ain't going anywhere. He knows we'll come in and clobber him if he makes a move. He's not stupid."

"What do we care about them? That's a world away. Oceans in between."

"Tom wouldn't risk his fields with any damn fireworks. Might be a band though. Sandy said she saw a fellow with a fiddle get off the bus yesterday and start walking towards town."

"I've heard if it does happen, we'll have to pay more for food, because ships are gonna get caught up in the mess of it all."

"It ain't idle speculation neither."

"Saw them kissing in Del's. Right there at the front counter as if there weren't no one around. Del'd gone around back to see what he'd ordered for the Meller boy. I was just coming in the store, the bell ringing on the door and everything, but it was nothing to them. They kept right at each other, hands in each others hair, bodies fit together like they was meant to. I just walked right on out. I

didn't want to break that up. I could get some roofing nails any old time. Walked right on home."

"Why won't you tell me what's happening tonight, Samuel? What's the big secret? Have you heard what people are saying?"

"It's no secret, Amelia. I truly don't know. My father is keeping the whole festivity very close to the chest. Any time I walk into a room, he and my mother clam up and stop talking. It's like they're planning a war or something."

"What about you? Do you have anything planned I should know about?"

So she had heard all the rumors. Who had let it slip that he intended to propose to her after the party? Samuel did not have many good friends in town, but had felt the need to get it off his chest, so he had let it slip to some school friends. It had not been enough to hear Eddard Morley's congratulations in writing. He needed a live body to tell him he was making the right decision. Part of Samuel had always known that the word would get out, that by telling anyone in town he was really telling the world what he intended to do. He had known this and had done it anyway. Samuel wanted to feel the pressure of expectations, of certainty. He was not scared. Amelia was the only woman he would ever love; of this he was as certain as any man can be.

"I plan to have a very good time. Don't you?"
"Of course I do, and to give you a nice gift."
"Just nice?"
"It's very nice."
"Well let's have it out then."
"Oh I don't think so. Your birthday isn't until tomorrow. Don't think I'll go and give up your gift a day early. You may be special, but not that special. You can wait like everyone else, young man."

Everyone else was indeed waiting for the party. The town seemed to be at a stand still on the first of September. The stores were nominally open, but no one was buying anything, and most folks were standing around in the aisles and in the booths and in the street, just talking in semi-circles about what might be in store for that night on the Meller property. They were all biding their time until eight o'clock rolled around when they would swamp the Meller property en masse to find out what Tom had whipped up for them.

At eight o'clock the town's residents found the Meller land lit up, their path to the barn easy to see as a line of torches stuck firmly in the ground burned a festive light, leading them towards the party. The well-lit path through the fallow fields cast eerie shadows on the ground, the flickering torches showing unfaithful silhouettes of those who walked by, unheeding of their shadows, ready to forget about their worries for an evening, and party on another man's dime, a man they so often criticized. It was Samuel's eighteenth birthday and it was time for the party to get started.

Folks were pouring in well past eight, and the barn began to fill. The punch bowls were emptied and then refilled, the kegs of beer were holding steady. The man of the hour watched once more from the loft that had been the home of a man named Eddard Morley for a year, Amelia at his side. They watched the revelling taking place in Samuel's name and smiled.

"I think Del's going to fall over," Amelia said. "He's swaying mightily."

"Oh no. He's got a few more glasses in him before he passes out in the field. I've seen him and my father drink together a few times, and the both of them can go well into the bottle."

"Why don't you have a drink? It's right and legal now."

"Bit on the nose isn't it?"

"Come on then," she said, holding out her hand. "You're having a beer."

Samuel watched Amelia make her way through the crowd, and while sitting up in the loft that had once housed Eddard Morley, he could not help but think of the last time he had sat in this loft, looking across the barn at a girl, laughably clueless about how to approach her. Eddard had egged him on, told him to live up to his life's desire to do something important. He had done it, and something important had happened, if very belatedly. His eyes unfocused, his mind elsewhere, Samuel lost track of Amelia in the crowd of his own raucous party. When his eyes came back into focus, and his attention was solely on the present, and it was not because of Amelia. It was because there was a great deal of shouting and commotion at the barn door. Some young men were shouting and whooping, while older men near them looked on somberly. The men shouted and the women whispered.

> *"It happened."*
> *"He moved."*
> *"Called the bluff."*
> *"I hope we don't get involved."*
> *"There's nothing else to be done."*
> *"We can't abandon them."*
> *"Hitler invaded Poland."*

Samuel looked frantically for Amelia but could not seem to find her in the crowd. She had been swallowed up into the mass of seething townspeople, and Samuel felt dizzy, out of control, and lost. He was falling down a well. Down. Down. Down he fell and he could see up only through a pinprick of light that was located directly at the center of his pupil. Where was Amelia?

It wasn't Amelia that woke Samuel, but his father.
"Up!"

Samuel was no longer in the loft, but on the barn floor below. He had evidently fallen from his perch and to the ground. He sat up painfully, but nothing was broken. His father's face was full of fright, anger.
"Where's Amelia?"
"She's fine. Get up. You need to help."
"Help what?"
Samuel's father hauled him up onto his legs and that was when Samuel noticed that there was less people around. Had his party ended? There were still crowds of young

men strewn about. Some of them were shouting, but not about Hitler or the war. They waved their arms at Tom Meller and he waved back, telling them to give him a second. Tom Meller slapped his son across the face, hard.

With a red hand mark still searing on his face, Samuel smelled the smoke. Something was burning. The barn was on fire.

"What"

"No time."

It would become clear later that in their haste and excitement, some young men had taken up the torches from the fields and carelessly left them lying about. A fire started and the dry September air had done the rest. By the time they reached the outside of the bar, Samuel realized that his father had not been making a choice by waking him. The barn was going to collapse, and everyone else had forgotten about the birthday boy in all of the ruckus. A line of men was carrying buckets from the Meller water pump, the bravest of these mounting ladders against the burning barn to try and extinguish the flame where it was the hottest. For the second time in his life, Samuel found himself useless in a life or death situation with the old barn. He sat on his haunches in the fields, trying to get his bearings. His ears were yet ringing and his head was pounding. He watched as his father, Del, and the others worked to fight the fire that wouldn't quit. In a moment of spectacular melancholy, fireworks began to shoot from the collapsing barn, climbing high into the air and raining down an unearned celebration on the sweating, sooty men. Samuel looked up in amazement and admiration of what his father had done for him. One after one, the fireworks went up, the delayed boom of their explosions adding a dramatic flare to the steady blaze the men battled. Tom Meller looked back to see stars in his son's concussed eyes, his boy as ever, able to see wonder where nobody else could. The men worked on, giving little notice to the display going on above their heads. Children miles away were probably enjoying the show, having no clue the carnage the lighting sparks of their joy was causing.

It was late in the night when Tom Meller made the decision to give up the barn for lost. He had the men make a perimeter around the barn, a moat of sorts. They took their buckets and made a circle around the barn, wetting the ground as much as they could, making sure that the fire could not travel any farther. Any attempts to save the barn were abandoned, and all the energy was focused on containment. Samuel watched in horror, his mind starting to come back around, his whole body beginning to ache. The barn collapsed in on itself. No braces cut from trees in the south wood could keep it from falling this time. A blackened ruin, it fell with with exhaustion, a heap of ashes on the ground, a few shards of unburned wood sticking up like skeletal, disapproving hands from an unfinished grave.

"Welcome to manhood," Tom Meller said to his son, sitting down next to him in the field.
The older man's face was covered in soot, his hands were cut and bleeding, and a patch of his pants were burned,

showing the discolored skin beneath. He put his arms around his son and held him.

"So this is it?" Samuel said.

"This is it."

"You could have saved the barn."

"I wanted to, son. I wanted to. But no, I couldn't have saved the barn. I knew it was gone."

"Then why even try?"

"This is it, Samuel," Tom said, standing up wearily. "Let's go to bed."

"I don't want to."

"Let's go to bed. And you're seeing the doc in the morning. Up."

Samuel listened to his father, but could not stop himself from looking over his shoulder at where the barn should have been. It was really gone. What if there were more vagrants? What if someone needed to use the barn for something? Where would parties be hosted? All these questions and more seemed up the utmost importance to Samuel, and as if they needed to be answered right at that moment. He would have to wait at least until morning.

13

In the morning, in town to see the doctor, no one seemed to care that the Meller barn had burned down. The talk of the town from the day before had faded quickly away. Only a few were willing to talk about the party. What was a local barn fire when Europe was on fire? It had finally begun in earnest. The talk of the United States' role in the war was renewed. A young man who worked behind the pharmacy counter was talking loudly on the porch to anyone who would listen.

"I'll sign up as soon as they let us know. Our country ain't going to fight the Nazis without me."

"Useless bit of a promise," Samuel spat.

"What do you know about it, Meller? Going to fight the war from your dormitory? Gonna throw a volume of Dickens at the Germans?"

"No, but I'll do better than you. I'm going to join the Eagles in England. I'll be fighting the Germans while you're still out here yammering for whoever's stupid enough to sit around and listen to you."

"Think your head go knocked a bit too much, Meller. You're talking out your ass. Or should I say arse?" There was a peal of laughter from the pharmacy porch, and Samuel let it go. He still had a headache and didn't fancy standing around trading words with such an idiot. But he had meant what he said. The words out of his mouth had not been planned, but as soon as they left his lips they had become true. He knew that he would follow through. It was his moment. Surely it was a sign that Hitler had made his move on Samuel's eighteenth birthday. That must mean it was time for him to make his mark on history, to help defeat the Germans, to whip them before his American friends were even called on.

"His mind's been addled," his mother said when he came home to declare his intentions. "You need to recover, dear. Come and lie down."
"Nothing's wrong with my head. Doc said I was fine. The headache will subside and there shouldn't be any lasting damage."

"Well there will be lasting damage if you go and get yourself blown up," Blynne screeched. "Tom, talk sense to him."

"Your mother is right. You can't be serious. You're probably a little shaken up. A lot has happened in a short amount of time. Take a moment to think about what you're saying, what you're committing too. Think on Amelia."

Tom Meller had hit on Samuel's greatest fear about his decision. Amelia had promised to wait for him while he was in college, but would she wait for him if he went to England?

"She'd be crazy to let you go off like this," his mother said. "And I'd not blame her. If you go, I'll tell her to marry someone else myself. If you love that girl, you'll not go."

"Then you know nothing of love," Samuel said. "I love her, and I have to go. I feel both of these things deeply."

"That's the problem with folks your age. Too much deep feeling. Your brain haven't calmed down enough to match your adult bodies."

"Samuel," Tom said. "Your mother is right, and you ought to apologize to her for what you've said. You can't leave a woman you love this way. It's one thing getting called to war, it's a whole different thing to go of your own accord. That's no better than glory-seeking. It's not duty. Don't get them confused."

"And what about moral duty? What about that? Am I meant to listen to radio reports of death and destruction while I study Proust? Is it not my moral obligation to act in accordance with my own values, and not the values espoused by our chickenshit government?"

"Your moral obligation is to Amelia, and to your family. You've never understood that."

"I understand it perfectly. I just don't believe it."

"Those books have made a thinker out of you," Tom said. "But not a man. You embarrass me. If you leave, don't you dare come back."

"Come back?" Samuel shrieked, his voice reaching a fever pitch. "What for? You think I want this plot of land? I've watched you slave at this place for eighteen years. Your back is bent. Your hands are ruined. Your face is lined. And you don't know anything. You've no time to learn. The only thing you'll ever know is how to farm. I don't want any part of this place. There's nothing lasting about it. Not a damn thing. It sickens me, and I'd be glad never to set foot here again."

"Samuel!" his mother cried. "Family. It's the-"

"That about the measure of how you feel?" Tom asked.

"Yes," Samuel said, between clenched teeth.

"I'll not be helping you with your bags."

Blynne began to weep when Samuel mounted the stairs to go to his bedroom and gather his things. "He's just a boy!" he heard her shrill. He had not intended for the conversation to go that way. He had not intended to say such terrible things to his father and mother that he did not truly believe. But he was too proud to take them back, and Tom Meller was too proud to ask him to. Samuel had spit on his father's entire existence and there was no going back on a thing like that. An apology could be made, but those words could not be unsaid.

In his room, he rolled his clothes slowly, choosing only a small pack to take with him. How does one pack to leave a place for the final time? So rarely does a man know when the last time he'll set foot in a place is, and so rarely is he given an opportunity to think it over in real time. In the end, he chose his clothes more or less at random, and three books, paperbacks to save weight, before tying his bag's straps and swinging it over his shoulder. His mother clung to him in the front room, begging him to stay. His father was nowhere to be seen.

"He didn't mean it," Blynne said. "He didn't mean it. You don't have to go. You two have never seen eye to eye. Go and apologize to him. He didn't mean it." Samuel extricated himself wordlessly from his mother, squeezing her one last time and kissing the top of her head.

"Yes he did. Only, he's never had the courage to say it before."

With that, the young man was out the door. He did not immediately leave the Meller property, as there was a place he needed to say goodbye too. The south wood had been his haven in a world unfamiliar and useless to him. He owed that place another afternoon, and he intended to spend his last time on the Meller property in its best places. He walked about the woods alone for the first time in what seemed ages. Rare had it been in recent years that he had gone about the south wood without Amelia at his side, her hand intertwined with his, asking him kindly to talk about a tree or a flower he had long since explained to her.

"I just like the sound of your voice," she said. "Tell me again."

His last time in the wood, Samuel began to cry. His head ached and his body was sore from his fall. His mind was whirring and the reality of his choices were beginning to set in. He looked around him and began to speak out loud to himself. The black alder, native to Europe, its origins in the south wood of the Meller property unknown. A tree that thrives in moist soil, growing up to a hundred feet. He ran his hand along the trunk, feeling the moss that depended on the tree for its life. Whenever his father wanted to smoke meats, Samuel had brought in some fresh alder branches, their dark, wet consistency giving an unforgettable flavor to the meat. Around and around he went, from plant to tree to rock, reminiscing or speaking out loud to himself as if Amelia were there to listen, to hear him pour out every memory of the wood that he could muster in his attempt to save the place forever, to stamp it on his memory indelibly so that he could not forget it. Samuel had read enough that he had begun to forget books he had read years before. Their pages faded from him slowly unless refreshed with another reading, the words losing their meaning, becoming only blocks of text on a page that had once held his attention in some important way. The forest was receding from his memory already, even as he stood within it. In fact, he had singularly acted to speed it up. He was eighteen years old, and his life had not just begun. It had been long, and full. But it was about to begin anew. Samuel was afraid.

The walk to the Fribley's house was the longest of his young life. It was not far from the Meller's, just in town. The Fribley's did not own a telephone, so there was little chance any news of Samuel's departure from home had reached Amelia yet. He needed to tell her himself, to ask her to honor her promise to wait for him. She had once told him it would be her honor to wait for him, and now he needed her to wait. His mother had said she would be a fool to do so, and Samuel could only hope that Amelia would not feel the same way. His love for Amelia was vast, but he could not help but notice she had disappeared from his mind while the pharmacy counter boy had been speaking. Nothing but a blind rage had filled Samuel, a rage that built and offered its own solution, such an obvious solution, but it was not one that included any consideration of Amelia. Could he now ask this of her, when he had not considered her during his own decision making? Was he not asking too much? Could he blame her for letting him go?

Samuel did not know the answer to such questions, and he would not for many years, but he could not leave without at least asking her to put her heart on hold, to allow him to do what he felt he was called to do. He remembered the night before. She had asked him if there was any surprise she should be ready for. The ring rested at the bottom of his pack, but he could not tell her about it. Things had changed since last night. Everything had changed. The ring was from a simpler world and a simpler time. He still wanted to give it to her, but it was no longer the time.

He could not live with himself for leaving, nor could he live with himself if he chose to stay. Remaining stagnant was a choice in itself; Samuel chose the path of action. He knocked on the door, waiting for Amelia to appear. Samuel shuffled his feet and adjusted the straps of his pack.

"Don't," she said, and nothing more, looking at him without pleading.

"I have to."

"Why?"

"I don't know."

"As good as nothing then. If you can't tell me what compels you to go, then it cannot be so compelling that you would leave me behind."

"You said you would wait for me."

"Don't twist my words, Samuel. I gave conditions. I am not yours by right, and I'll not stick by your side no matter what fool decision you make. Surely your books have taught you that no love is without conditions. Anyone who loves unconditionally is a fool. I'll not tear my hair out waiting to hear if you're dead. I won't."
They sat in the back garden of the Fribley home. It was a sad affair, weedy and neglected, the wooden boxes holding together the concept of "garden" that might otherwise have been considered merely a patch of ground.

"You can't mean that."

"What do you want me to say?"

"That you don't mean it."

"I do. I love you. I'll not deny it, but I can love another. You show me no love in return by leaving me without reason. Have you no sense of duty?"

"My duty calls me away."

"Not duty, vanity."

Her words were a slap across Samuel's face. She knew him better than anyone, understood him far better than his father or mother ever had, and she cut to the core of him easily, like it was nothing.

"Whatever you want to call it, I can't deny it. I know I have to go."

"Then you do not love me."

"I love you, but I also-"

"Don't you dare," she snapped. "Don't you dare compare me to that war, to your duty, to whatever it was you meant to say. Don't dare and do it. Such comparisons are the refuge of sad, pathetic men."

"You think I'm pathetic?"

"You don't love me. I'm just a girl who was across the barn. It could have been anyone else."

"It couldn't have."

"It will be."

Silence enveloped the two of them. There was a soft breeze, but nothing grew hardily enough in the Fribley's garden to sway in the wind. All dead stocks and sweaty weeds to heavy to be moved.

"I'll come back."

"I'll not wait for you. Not for this."

"I'll not forget you."

Samuel left the Fribley's with his pack slung over one shoulder and his body feeling as heavy as it ever had. Decisions had been made, and now the consequences would have to be faced. Samuel was going to the biggest city he could get to, and was going to find his way to England.

Part 2:

1

Even then, folks didn't think of Cleveland in the same breath as New York, Boston, or San Francisco, but to Samuel's mind it was the best option at hand, and one to which he could afford the bus fare out of pocket. The beginning of his second life accorded appropriately with his mood. It was rainy, the bus was leaky, and his fellow passengers were smelly vagabonds. Samuel had not yet reached the point where he considered himself one with his fellow passengers. In reality, he had quit his past life resolutely, declining options to return given to him by numerous parties. Still, he felt buoyed above his fellow travellers by the comfort and status of his old life. He did not literally expect anyone to offer him deference, but Samuel still carried himself as a privileged child might. It takes more than a personal decision to rid oneself of privilege. Oftentimes, the objective cruelty of the outside world is required.

The bus bumped along, and the rain fell incessantly, a small drip falling directly onto Samuel's knee, no matter how he squirmed in his attempted sleep. After seventy two and one half hours, Samuel was deposited on Euclid avenue in the middle of the night. It wasn't raining, but the air stank of a recent bout of it, and the gutters ran heavy. He was able to find a room without too much difficulty. It overlooked the river if you squinted hard enough, but Samuel didn't care. His bag as a substitute for the paltry pillow on the hotel bed, he fell to the sagging mattress and passed out.

When he woke, the city was alive with activity. It was close to midday, and though Cleveland was hardly the Big Apple, the amount of folks walking about, and cars honking and spewing smoke on the street when Samuel lifted up the blinds was still hard to believe for a farm boy like Samuel. It was in the face of this perceived hubbub that the country boy was forced to reckon with the first and most obvious flaw in his reckless plan to leave home in search of military glory. He had not the first idea how to volunteer for the royal army, and the crowds of people below him did nothing to encourage his already flagging sense of purpose. The young man force himself to get up and splash cold water on his face. His room provided a sink, but the bathroom was public. He scratched at his teeth with his nails and examined himself in the mirror. He looked like an eighteen year old boy, but his farm upbringing was to his advantage. He was more tan, and more lean than most boys his age, and looked (truthfully) as if he would have no problem doing a day's labor. His round, steel glasses rested on his nose unflatteringly to his mind, but there was little that could be done about that.

In a rookie move, Samuel left his bag on the hotel bed, locked the door behind him, and headed down the street to use what was left of the day to his advantage. He wasn't certain where to begin, but it was to be his lucky day. Not seven blocks away, he ran into an army recruiter. The officer, believing Samuel wanted to join the army, was very forthcoming and willing to talk. Once the truth came out, he was less so.

"Why would you want to do a fool thing like that?"
"They'll need all the help they can get."
"So will we."
"Maybe so."
"You're trading in on your own country on that evidence?"
"Sir, I'm not doing anything of the sort. I just want to do my part to fight Hitler. I've had a premonition that it's what I have to do."
"Hurry to die, are you?"

"No, sir."
"Polite, aren't you?"
"Sir."
"You're serious about this?"
"I can put you in contact with somebody, but I can't make any guarantees."
"Really?"

The man's change of heart came as a surprise to Samuel.

"Meet me back here at 1500 hours."
"Yes, sir."

Samuel walked on air all the way back to his hotel room, and even had a difficult time putting the key in the lock when he returned, so shaky were his hands in his excitement. His excitement quickly abated once he saw his room. It was just as he had left it, with one small exception: his bag was no longer on his bed. In fact, his bag was nowhere to be found. He sprinted down the hotel stairs, taking three or four at a time until he stood at the front desk, panting.

"My bag is gone," he said breathlessly to the old woman at the desk.

"I'll call the constable."

"Okay."

The woman emitted a rasping, shaking set of breaths that could only have been her version of laughing. She slapped the counter gently.

"You're an earnest one."

"I don't understand."

"Well I'll make it real easy for you. There's no constable, and you should read better."

The old woman pointed to a sign tacked to the wall above the cutout in the wall that allowed her to converse with customers. The skin on her elbow swung pendulously, but Samuel tore his eyes from her paper-thin skin to read the sign. It read, simply: Hotel Assumes No Responsibility for Lost Items.

"It's not lost. It was stolen."

"Oh, he's a nitpicker. We don't recognize any distinction there. Best of luck to you."
She turned to go.
"My whole life was in that bag."
She paused for an almost imperceptible moment, but no she did not turn around. Her hardened sense of justice could only be melted so far. This lad needed to learn to keep his wits about him, or he'd never make it. Let him learn his lesson this time.

Samuel returned to his room and sat on the sagging mattress. At this time, as he did at so many other times in his life, he wanted to speak to Eddard Morley. He thought of writing to him on the bus, but had changed his mind. Samuel was yet to admit it to himself, but he was afraid that Eddard might disapprove of his actions. He feared such an outcome. For all his show of independence and fate, Samuel still feared the reproval of the old vagabond. Samuel's personal history bore out the correctness of the old man on a number of occasions, and he couldn't bare to be told that his life epiphany which had caused him to leave everything behind, including the woman he loved and his family, was fraudulent or rash in some way. It was too late now. The deed had been done and could not be undone as easily as admitting it had been wrong. So, Samuel thought of Eddard as the sound of slamming car doors, shouting hot dog vendors, and general noise came in from the window. At least, he thought, he would not be late to his meeting with the man from the royal army, because the building directly across from his room was topped by a massive clock that chimed every half hour.

Samuel was early to his meeting and the recruiter, who introduced himself this time as Sergeant Corden in accordance with his name on his uniform, seemed pleased with Samuel's timeliness.

"Deborah should be here shortly."
"Deborah?"
"A nurse, son. Medical exam. You pass that, then you can talk to a Sergeant who's gathering volunteers."
"What's the exam for?"

"You hard of hearing? It's a medical exam."

"Shouldn't they take anyone they can get?"

"You're really inspiring confidence there, boy. I'll run that up the flagpole and see what my superiors think of cutting out our medical clearances. The short answer is no. A soldier unfit to fight is a danger more to his comrades than to himself. That's why."

The sergeant had some paperwork to do, and Samuel found himself alone again. If there was one thing his life up until this point had prepared him for, it was being alone. Although he much preferred being alone in the south wood to the city, he could handle it. He found himself in another hotel lobby, one that was average, but by that metric still far superior to the one in which he was staying. He sat on a divan close to the center of the room and looked about. There were a few men sitting in chairs drinking coffee, a short line to speak to the desk clerk who, smiling and gracious appeared more as a desk clerk should than the old woman with the pendulous arm skin. A young couple argued while a baby cried on his mother's hip. Some chocolate was smeared across the baby's face, and the high pitched ringing of a phone was incessant.

Samuel sat with his hands in his lap, staring at his brown boots until a hand rested on his shoulder. He looked up to see a woman in a nurse's uniform, a shapely girl with a gap tooth looking down on him.

"Sergeant Corden described you. You the one I'm looking for?"

"You aren't English."

"Observant enough. Up with you. They let me do this in a room on the first floor. Let's go."

She lead him to a small room to which she produced a key from her bosom. She instructed him to take off his shirt and sit on the bed.

"I didn't mean to be rude," Samuel said. "I was only surprised."

"It's extra money," she said plainly. "Sergeant Murray pays us American girls well. They don't want to have to bring their own over for this. Cough."

She stood up and pulled a card from her back pocket, holding it up at her shoulder level.

"Over by the desk. Now take off your glasses."

"What for?"

"A pissing contest. Jesus, kid. Take off your glasses."

Samuel did as he was told. She asked him to recite what was on the bottom line of the card she held. He was of course, unable to do so with any accuracy.

"You can put 'em back on hon."

"What's next?"

"Nothing. You're blind as a bat."

"So does that change what posting I might get?"

"No posting. You failed."

"I don't understand."

"Not much to understand really. We're looking for pilots. Pilots have to see. Those are the rules. Go home, kid. Make babies. You'll be happier for it."

Samuel grabbed the nurse by the shoulder.

"Please, you don't understand."

She removed his hand from her shoulder with a look of utter revulsion.

"I'm not the one who needs to come to an understanding here."

With that, she was gone, and Samuel was alone in a hotel room, the clothes on his back the only thing to his name, his plan dashed within a day, feeling increasingly foolish with every passing moment. He couldn't let it go so easily.

He returned to the lobby and waited for the sergeant to show himself again. It took hours, and Samuel's stomach was growling, the sun setting outside, but eventually he showed himself again. Samuel accosted him and began speaking at once.

"Slow down, kid. What do you want? I set up the exam for you, which is more than I should have done."

"I need to see the sergeant in person, to explain my situation. I need to make him understand."

"Deborah will talk to him for you. In due time. Don't rush it."

"She said I failed, but-"

"You failed? Well then what are you talking about?"

"I need to talk to the sergeant."

"You need to go home. Listen, I've got a dinner. I've got to go. Good luck, kid."

Samuel was left to face a hard truth: he had rushed from home without planning enough, and the worst had happened. It did not change his intuition that he had been meant to leave, was being called away by the war, but he had badly misfired. In his lowest moment, that evening as the kind desk clerk informed him he would have to leave the lobby, and he began to walk the streets of Cleveland by night, he thought of Amelia. His mind traveled back to the first time in the car, the rain on the windshield, how they had argued, but he had never felt so alive. He thought of his party, which now seemed eons in the past, searching for her in the crowd of people from the vantage point of the loft. He hadn't been able to locate her. He had tried, but he never saw her in the crowd, never found her, locked eyes, promised. Then it had all come crashing down in fire. It seemed so long ago he had laid in the field and seen the fireworks and the ash of the old barn, crumbling slowly beneath the brightly lit explosions. It had not been so long, but everything had changed.

Defeated and exhausted, Samuel only just made it back to his room. He collapsed on the bed for the second consecutive night and fell into a deep sleep filled with troubling dreams.

Things did not get better for Samuel in the morning, as he was booted from his room by the angry old woman for failing to pay up for another day. It was all the same, as it would have been a waste of precious little money he had left that had not been in his stolen bag. Nothing else to do, Samuel walked the streets aimlessly, thoughtlessly moving downhill as it was easier on his legs. Eventually, he found himself at water level with the Cuyahoga, throwing railroad rocks into the dark water. He came across a bar, and though it was morning time, he went inside. It was dark, and Samuel supposed, dark as the river was, even if there had been windows, the place would have been dreary. It suited his mood just fine. He sat at the bar and told the man who tended it to make his choice for him.

"My own brew," the bartender said proudly. "Calling it beech leaf brew. See the engraving on the glass there."

Samuel nodded, and nearly every part of his exhausted body wanted him to end the interaction right there, but his old self was still in there. The youth who read Thoreau with such voracity, and who thought of himself as a naturalist, couldn't let it go.

"Ought to call it chestnut brew."

"Not much of a ring to it."

"Well that's what this leaf favors," Samuel said, indicating the engraving. "Good though. Much thanks."

"What's the difference between a chestnut leaf and a beech leaf?"

"Not a lot, other than coming from different trees."

Samuel hadn't meant anything by it, but it was clear that he had offended the bartender, who had been kind enough to share his home brew. He turned his back on Samuel and polished some glasses with undue gusto.

A man approached the bar and sat down next to Samuel. He was older, but hard looking, deeply cut lines in his face, and wore an out of fashion slouch hat back on his crown. He was chewing on a cigar that looked as if it hadn't been lit in the past century, and had a white beard that covered all but his eyes, mouth, and nostrils.

"Mind if I sit?"
"Plenty of room."
"Like trees?"

It was an odd question to be sure, but considering the exchange with the bartender, understandable in context. And Samuel was feeling down, vulnerable, mostly just waiting for someone to spill his guts to. This man had evidently volunteered himself.

"If I have any religion, it rests in trees."

"That's a hell of a thing for a young man to say. Lot of years left for you to find religion."

"I told you, I've already found it. Call it religion if you like, I don't know what to call it."

"Not a lot of men who can tell the difference between a beech and a chestnut leaf. Look damn near the same."

"Pretty easy to tell when they're on the tree." At this the man laughed, taking his cigar stub out of his mouth to release the air from his belly. He patted Samuel on the back, though the young man hadn't intended a joke. It seemed that no one in this city could tell when he was joking.

"True enough. Do you mind, boy if I ask you a question?"

"Shoot."

"You a bit down this morning?"

"What gave it away?"

"Looking for a change?"

"I'm not going to work on any railroad if that's what you're aiming at."

"Oh no," he said. "Far from that. But it seems to me like I've run into you for a reason. You see, I'm looking for someone like you. Hard at times like these. Most men are preparing for the war, least those who haven't deluded themselves into thinking there won't be one."

"War doesn't want me. I've got bad eyes."

"You ought to be thankful for that. That's not the suitor you should be aiming for. Your glasses fix you up?"

"Not well enough for fighting."

"Lot of things can happen in fighting, but I reckon you can see just fine when you're composed."

"What're you on about? Of course I can."

"Well enough to distinguish beech from chestnut anyhow."

"I'm nearly done with my beer."

"Another on me to hear me out."

"Fair."

The old man called the bartender over and ordered the beer.

"Name's Morgan," he said. "Alistair Morgan. I work for the National Parks Service and we're worried about the war."

"Join the club. I don't suppose most people have the parks at the top of their worries list when it comes to Hitler."

"Right you are, but that doesn't make it less of my job. I've a sense of duty. I won't be a soldier. I'm too old, but we're about to face a crisis. A lack of warm bodies, and I've been sent out to try and solve it. Now, you can't fight Hitler, but we'll take you. You'll still be doing good."

"What do you want me to do?"

"Be a fire lookout. It's a young man's job, and our young men are about to be lost to a different cause. Fires don't stop because we're at war. Job still needs filling. And it seems to me that I've run into just the man for the job. You have an appreciation for nature, you're young, and as far as I can tell, have got nothing else going on."

"You're very observant, Mr. Morgan. What's the pay?"

"Bad, but the views are good."

It was Samuel's turn to laugh.

"I imagine there's a lot of time for a man to reflect."

"More than you probably want."

"I've got a lot to reflect on."

"More than you probably want."

"So where's an opening?"

"Interested already? Am I so good a salesman?"

"Like you said, I've not got much going on, and that was an understatement. I'd not get too many ideas about your skills as a salesman."

"Southern Appalachians. Shuckstack lookout is currently being filled by a part timer."

"I don't know where that is."

"North Carolina, son. Beautiful country."

"You really think we're going to join the war?"

"You've got your own war to worry about now. Uniform is pretty lax though."

2

Maybe it was his purpose all along, or just dumb luck. Either way, Samuel was game to let himself be swept away. It only seemed appropriate that his own particular war was to be against fire. He knew a thing or two about that. With a fifty dollar advance and his train fare paid for, Samuel's life took an abruptly formal turn. He had a purpose and a destination. He was expected to report to the interim lookout at Shuckstack, a man named Milton, in no more than ten days. His trip via train to Bryson City, North Carolina would take him no more than three days, but there was little keeping Samuel in Cleveland. He did stop at the library to find out a little bit about the place he was going to call home. He was not disappointed by the grainy photos in the books: the beauty of the place was clear to see. The tower itself was a public works project from Roosevelt, and it stood more than four thousand feet from sea level. It overlooked thousands of miles of the Smoky Mountains, which were all a part of Samuel's lookout domain.

"Job's simple enough," Samuel had been told over his free beer. "If you can see smoke or fire, you report, and then investigate if possible. In that order. If you can see it, it falls under your purview. Your workplace is thousands of miles of rough country. I want you to understand that. This isn't a picnic you're signing up for. You aren't going to be in any army, but don't think you'll be lounging."

Samuel had been told that in the wet seasons, he was free to stay in the tower, but he had do best to save his wages whatever he chose to do.

"Most men go home. See their folks. Take in some conversation with other living people."

"I'll not go home."

"We'll see about that after you spend some time up there alone. Solitude's good for a man, but not every man can take what's good for him after so long."

Samuel went up to the circulation desk and requested a library card so that he could check out the book about

Shuckstack tower, and a few other books about flora and fauna in the smoky mountains. He figured on reading them on the train. He told himself he'd return the books eventually. On the inside flap, it indicated that none of the books had been checked out in years. He hoped not to be depriving anyone of a pleasure. His books under his arm, he went in search of some clothes. He had been advised to buy clothes before the train arrived in Bryson City. He purchased some heavy, brown pants, good, rain-proofed boots, and two, thick flannels. On a whim, he bought himself a brimmed cap. He'd never been one to wear hats, but this one struck his fancy. It was gray and had a brown leather band all the way around it: one piece, no buckle holding it together. He bought a traveler's rucksack to shove his new clothes and library books in, and bought a few trashy, adventure books to read once he got tired of the more scholarly texts.

With his ticket in hand, his rucksack on the bench next to him, Samuel Meller waited on the train and reflected on all that had happened that lead him to this place of all places.

A train station in Cleveland, headed to the heart of the Smoky mountains to look for fire. It seemed to him that fire marked his coming into this man's world. Fire had marked his eighteenth birthday, and fire was to be his calling. He thought of Amelia in spite of himself. The resoluteness of her face as she told him she would not wait for him. It was the same resolute attitude that he had found when he had foolishly told her how much he wanted to leave their town on that first evening they had spoken, Eddard Morley pushing him on. Samuel cursed himself twice over. Once for letting his mind wander to Amelia, and once for forgetting to buy pen and paper. He hoped that there would be some available in Bryson City. His wandering thoughts had lead him to Eddard Morley, as they often did. He had put off writing a letter to Eddard out of fear, but it was time to come clean of it and tell the old man everything that had happened recently. Samuel felt more beholden to the old man's opinion than just about anyone else. It was strange. Samuel and Eddard had only truly been friends for a few weeks when they lived on the same property, but Samuel felt closer to Eddard the more the years passed, the longer in between letters they had gone. It was as if the distance between them drew them closer together in Samuel's mind. There was something natural to that sort of relationship. Writing letters back and forth seemed to Samuel to be just about the most accurate way of communicating with anybody. You've got time to work out just what it is you really want to say. So much hurt in the world caused by bad momentary judgment that could easily be allayed by simply never having intimate conversation. Samuel knew his relationship with his father would certainly be better if they had spent their entire lives in utter silence, but exchanged lengthy letters expounding upon their views. Surely then, Tom Meller would begin to understand his only son.

Lost in his thoughts and half-imagined truths, Samuel nearly missed his train. It took the warning whistle to wake him from his wakeful stupor, eyes staring vacantly from the bench, straight through the departing train. His ticket was punched from the steps.

"Saw you sitting there while we was boarding. What, you just like a little giddy up is that it?"

"I've never been on a train before."

"But you did know youse supposed to board them before they start moving."

"I do now, sir."

The most notable change Samuel had ever observed in real time occurred out the window of the train. He watched, mesmerized and unable to look away as the flattened Midwest he was so accustomed to gave way to southern stub pines, rock faces, and enough ups and downs to pop his ears ten times over. He happily worked his jaw up and down and felt as his temples as he kept his eyes glued to the window. It was a country he'd only read about. He reckoned that folks his own age were shortly going to be fighting for this land, and they'd probably never seen it before either. Hell, he'd never been within a few thousand miles of England, and he'd been just about to fight for them. Samuel could hardly believe this was the same country in which he had grown up. Here was a place surely

as foreign as any part of China. He dug into his rucksack
and worked furiously at the pages of his library book to try
and identify trees as they went by. Mostly they went by too
fast, but ones that were most common he was able to dog
ear in the book. (He'd fix those before returning the book
to the library.) He saw holly, some towering and squat
magnolias, dogwoods in bloom, and at least three species
of pine that he could identify. He saw the loblolly, its
branches held out like a mother trying to stop two children
running in opposite directions, the digger pine, slanted and
unsure which direction to grow, and the creeping needles
of the long leaf pine. He saw piles of black walnuts at the
base of a tree close enough to the tracks that if his window
opened, he could have claimed a green, unripe walnut for
his own. Tossed into the mix were a few laurel, even a
naked sycamore, creeping towards the grave, soon to be
either firewood or detritus and dust. Samuel could hardly
fathom how similar and yet entirely different the terrain
was. He felt the same in his gut as he did when he walked
through the south wood of the Meller property, but the
makeup of the land was entirely different. These trees had

been described to him by writers, but had never been more than words on a page, descriptions of forms like Socrates pointing aimlessly up to the sky.

Not until the sun went down and his view was taken away did Samuel pull himself away from the window and back to the reality of the train. He paid fifty cents, a most unreasonable sum he felt, for a nearly inedible meal, and spent the early evening reading some more about Shuckstack Tower and the surrounding lands. He fell asleep with the book in his lap and woke up to sunlight streaming through the window, his book at his feet.

He rubbed the sleep out of his eyes and found them greeted by steep, mountain terrain.

"Them's the smokies," the ticket man said, come by again to punch Samuel's ticket. "Hard to tell real fire from the fog of the mountain sometimes."
"I ought to practice then."
"Why's that?"

"I'm to be a fire lookout."

"You?" the man said, as if the very look of Samuel made the idea of him being a fire lookout preposterous. "Ought to bring you another meal. You'll need some more meat on those gangly bones of yours. Wait til I've made my rounds."

The ticket man was strange, but delightfully unbothered by his own strangeness. As promised, he brought Samuel another meal for free, and sat across the aisle from him, rolled his own cigarette against his chest, and struck a match.

"Runnin from the war?"

"Excuse me?"

"I said, runnin from the war?"

"There's no war."

"Good answer, young man. Woodley's my name."

He offered his hand. Samuel took it and shook firmly.

"Samuel."

"Spent any time in the smokies before?"

"Not a moment."

"Best place in the world, I've always thought. Useless country for most of man's work, which makes it just about the most wonderful kind of place if you ask me. Soils full of rocks and the best trees are too hard to get to. Don't get me wrong. Some smart, city boy is going to figure out how to destroy it, but I'll be gone by then won't I?" He said, taking a long drag on his cigarette and holding it between his teeth. He pulled a stoppered bottle from his inside jacket pocket and took a swig. Samuel took a pull when it was offered, and gulped down the corn liquor that felt hot in his chest.

"I don't know about all that, but I'm going to try and make sure it doesn't all burn down."

"Damndest thing isn't it?"

"What?"

"Things we get up to. Government's paying you to watch for fires. Who you think did that before men were here? I'll tell you who: nobody. Sometimes things are just meant to burn."

"You just told me how wonderful the country is. You want me to let it burn?"

"You misunderstand me, son. I think what you're doing's about as good a calling as a man can get. Was only speaking on man's foibles more generally. If a man fights a losing battle his whole life, there's something worthwhile in that. Only think it's worth pondering that we even try. If you believe the leather bound book it's all going to flames anyway."

"I'm not much for religion," Samuel said.

"You might change your tune up on the mountain. Seen a few men in my time find religion up in the smokies. Few lost it too, so I s'pose it's all the same. What are you running from anyway? If it ain't the war, what is it?"

"Why've I got to be running?"

"Don't insult me, boy," he said, laughing and coughing. He stubbed out his cigarette under his boot, pulling out more loose leaf to roll. "I work on a train. I know the face of a man that's running, and you've got it."

"Well, how much time have you got?"

The man checked his watch.

"Enough."

So, Samuel gave the man his whole story. The whole damn thing. He started with when Eddard Morley and the vagrants came to town and worked all the way up to the present. The whole while, the old man did nothing but smoke his home rolls down to nubs, drink his corn liquor and occasionally tug on his hat. When Samuel was finished, he was ready to hear the man chastise him, but it didn't come.

"Hell of a story. You tell it well."

"You don't aim to tell me I'm making the biggest mistake of my life?"

"Wasn't going ta. You may want to consider why those are on the tip of your own tongue though. Ponder on that. Not my place to tell you what to do. You're old enough to get ripped and old enough to die in a trench, so far as I'm concerned we're on a footing here. Your choices are just that."

"Have you ever done something you've regretted?"

"Course. But so has every last soul on this train. You can't live with that in mind or you'll lose it fast. Long as you own the consequences of your choice, it'll be fine.

Doesn't mean you'll always make the right ones, but if there weren't consequences then it wouldn't be a choice anyway...I'm drunk."

"I appreciate the company. You drunk enough to give me your story? I gave you mine."

"Mine ain't nothing. I've been working on this train since I was nineteen years old. I was here on its first voyage cross the country. Been here ever since. Lived my whole life aboard just about."

The look on Samuel's face must have given him away as being shocked.

"You thought I was more than that?"

"I wouldn't quite put it like that."

"Sure you would. And you can. You thought I had a yarn to spin for you that lead me to this place. No, my life's momentum lead me here and then stopped. My choice."

"Why don't you do something else?"

"I like it here. It's a good job. Meet a lot of people. I like people. It suits me fine. I may just as well ask you why you didn't stay. Both are a choice."

A bell rang, and the ticket man swayed a little before standing up. From his belt he drew his puncher and punched Samuel's card once more. He gave the prospective fire lookout a tip of his cap and started walking back to the next car. Samuel followed him with his eyes. He saw the old man laughing with another passenger, his old face creasing at his lips and under his eyes. Wrinkles that had formed on the train, showed themselves to its passengers for the umpteenth time. No matter what the old man said, Samuel felt deeply, profoundly sad for him. What kind of life was that? Living on a train. It was the worst kind of sadness that gripped Samuel the rest of that day, because he had no reason to feel it. The man himself had not asked for sympathy, and had offered none in return. He was at peace with himself, and who was Samuel to feel secondhand grief for this man whose name he could no longer remember.

Getting off the train in Bryson City, Samuel found himself not yet to his destination. Upon inquiring the location of

Shuckstack Tower of the gas station attendant, he learned that the trail up the mountain began in Fontana Village, a full thirty miles away. The attendant jerked his thumb in the appropriate direction, and Samuel proceeded to stick his out on the side of the road, taking to his rucksack as a chair after an early afternoon of failure. Eventually, late in the afternoon, a truck stopped and indicated that he could ride in the back if it suited him.

"Holler when you want out," the man said.

Samuel thanked him and swung his rucksack into the back of the truck before climbing in himself. It was a spectacular country to see from the back of a truck, and Samuel enjoyed himself immensely, happy to let his hair blow in the breeze and to gaze out at the seemingly endless line of peaks and valleys. There was a sense of mystery to the mountains that Ohio was never able to bring. At the horizon line back home, it was easy to imagine what came next: another town, another car just over the hill. Out here, the peaks spoke to Samuel of places that men rarely traveled to, of sites that perhaps no one had even seen before. It looked so much bigger, the land intruding into the sky's territory in a way that never happened back home. At the first sign for Fontana Village, Samuel hollered and passed a dollar in through the truck window when the man slowed up enough for him to hop down. As the truck chugged away, Samuel hitched his rucksack up on his back, plopped his brown, brimmed hat on his head for the first time, and took his first steps as a mountain man.

It wasn't hard to find the trail that lead up the mountain, though the man at the convenience store whistled when he heard where Samuel was going.

"Hope you've got more than pencils and paper for that trip," he said, ringing up Samuel's purchases. "That's a hike. Cain't miss it though, they're fixing to dam the river. 'Nother Roosevelt's ideas. All sorts of government types hanging about town."

"It's a tough walk?"

"It's a hike, son. Not a walk. Elevation increases pretty rapidly. Tower's over four thousand high."

"Well, I better get started then."

The clerk nodded at him and smiled wryly. Samuel did not think his pack was heavy at first, and was enjoying his walk. It was solitary, and he stopped often: to watch a doe lead her babies a hundred yards off, their hoofs navigating a rocky outcropping better than Samuel could have managed, to pick flowers and put them delicately in his hatband, and to run his hands along the bark of trees as he liked to do so much back home in the south wood. As the walk wore on though, and the trail seemed to go on without ever getting closer to the top, his rucksack began to feel heavier, and his back was covered in sweat. The trail wove around and around in a zigzagging pattern up the mountain, far from a straightforward walk in the woods. At times, the trail was nothing more than a few feet from the edge of the world, and at other times Samuel found himself seemingly in the middle of the woods.

3

The air was cool at elevation, but his hat and shirt came off and were put away. The straps ate into his shoulders, and his boots were heavy, tripping over jutting roots of their own accord, sending Samuel stumbling upward at a terribly slow pace. It was beginning to get dark by the time the structure came into view. The tower was massive, standing another hundred feet above the elevated terrain. It stood on spindly, steel-bracings, with steps going all the way up, turned at right angles. He was disheartened to find that after the tower came into view, it disappeared just as quickly. The journey was not over. He was forced to wind through the mountains, occasionally getting a glimpse of his new home, it never seeming to get any closer. Eventually he reached the last quarter mile, the most perilously steep portion of all, and by this time he was too exhausted to not push through. After reaching the peak, Samuel sat down at the bottom of the tower for a while to gain his breath, next to the cabin that would be his home. Between the cabin, small and stone with a fireplace and a black, painted wood door, and the tower itself, there was hardly any other real estate on the peak. It could not have been more than a few hundred feet square. He sat with his pack up against the cabin and breathed the cool mountain air, looking out at the ridges in the distance, unmoving and archaic. Once he felt up to it, Samuel mounted the steps and counted them as he walked. He had reached seventy four when a voice reached him from the tiny, red wooden building that rested precariously atop the continuously swaying structure.

"You must be by new man."

"That I am."

"Come in and take a look around. I'll give you a moment before I start yammering. You'll need it."

As Samuel walked into the small space, he understood why he was being offered some time to take his bearings. The room itself was unspectacular, a radio on a small desk, a stack of books, a cot in the corner, and a not much else in the way of humanity. But what the room overlooked was spectacular. Windows encompassed three hundred and sixty degrees of the room, so that Samuel could see (though he knew not much of what he saw) great swaths of mountain country. To the west was the Unicoi range, the Nantahala to the south, the smokies east and north, and to the southeast the blue ridge peaks. Though Samuel could not put words to it, there was no need. Some things in life can only be seen, and though he loved them deeply, Samuel was starting to see the inherent uselessness of his beloved nature books. Clouds drifted in and out of his field of vision, a bird spinned and wheeled miles away, but clear as crystal to Samuel, right across his vision as if his nose was pressed to a tank containing all the wonders of the world.

"Everyone needs a moment, no matter who he is. Milton," he said, extending his hand. "Leroy Milton."

"Samuel Meller."

"Welcome to the best job on earth."

It didn't take long for Leroy Milton to run down the responsibilities of the job for the six "active" months. There wasn't much to it. The job description held nearly all the responsibilities right in it. He was first and foremost, a lookout. He watched for signs of fire, natural or otherwise. If smoke or other signs were spotted, he was to radio the ECC with approximate coordinates of the fire. Leroy Milton showed Samuel a handy system.

"Now stand at the tape line."
For the first time, Samuel looked down and noticed that there was tape put down about a foot from the wall, all the way around the 8x8 room.

"If you stand exactly at the tape line, and look out at the horizon, you'll notice I've marked certain points on the windows with a bit of fountain pen ink."

Samuel did as he was told, and sure enough, though they were minuscule and hard to see, there were dots of ink.

"In my logbook, which I'll leave with you, there's a diagram of all the windows with the points I've marked designated. It shows the coordinates of that spot. If something is near enough to the coordinate already marked, you can make a fairly steady estimation, otherwise...map it out and make a new notation. The man previous to me started this bit of ingenuity, and most of the marks are his own. He was a bit of an odd bird, but a genius. Evidently the service told him they'd give him a heliograph, but it never materialized and he came up with this rather than sit on his hands."

Samuel had to admit to the cleverness of the system, but was still yet to recover from the immensity of what could be seen from any point in the tower. Milton seemed to have moved on entirely, having given Samuel enough time to bask already.

"Your radio couldn't be simpler. It's just a two way. No jazz standards or Beethoven up here. Radio for that is in the cabin below. Anything you need, you talk to ECC, though don't go calling them if you have an ingrown nail. Just hold down this button here and speak your piece. There's always someone there, twenty-four seven, three sixty five. They're a part of this train that we're on too."

"So how long are you going to stay on?"

Leroy Milton laughed and patted Samuel on the back.

"I'm leaving in the morning, my friend. I suggest you give solitude some thought if you haven't already. Feels strange even having two people in this glass box. Especially when one of them isn't doing the common kindness of wearing a shirt."

"Oh, sorry it's just I got…"

"Let a man joke. I've not had an audience for a minute. You might as well leave it off now. Sun's going down and we'll need the light."

In spite of Leroy Milton's jab, there was an electric light in the glass box, a single bulb with a pull string just above where the cot was placed. Milton informed Samuel that as there was nowhere to store anything in the box, and not much more in the cabin. If he needed a new light bulb or to fix the radio, the five mile hike back down to the village would be a necessity.

"Long way for a light bulb."

"Long way from anything, yet look around you. Look how much you're close to. I didn't call it the best job in the world for nothing."

"Then why are you so excited to leave?"

"This ain't my post. I'm supposed to be your nearest neighbor, some fifty miles southeast in the blue ridge. It's empty right now, which isn't good. This was deemed higher priority."

Over a dinner eaten from tins, the two men got to know each other a little better. Leroy Milton offered no comment or criticism of Samuel's choices, only nodding at appropriate moments and sympathizing where necessary.

"I fought my war already," he said. "Was in France during the last one."

"What was it like?"

"Worst job in the world. No one should have to do it. As soon as I got my discharge papers I went home to the blue ridge and didn't talk another human being for something like two months. I'm not sure."

"Your family?"

"None to speak of. Parents died young, before the war. I was an ideal soldier, no next of kin, no letter needed to be typed out by a pool of typists with a form beside them. I'm solitary by nature. This job suits me. War is the opposite. It's all about people. They say sometimes that wars are about land, but it's never true. It's about the hurt feelings of some man or other, the land is just the excuse. That's the beauty of a place like this. There's no need to talk about it. For me, the blue ridge speaks for itself. Not my job to gush about stream pebbles and muskrat towers. The war was constant, unceasing human activity and I came to hate it more than I did before. They say killing is natural, but not like that. I've seen a fox take a rabbit from a hole, but that fox has to eat. That's human bullshit what happened in Europe, and it's human nonsense all over again. We were stuck in a hole in the ground, just waiting, sometimes shooting, sometimes moving ten feet further forwards to another hole. What for? Because some powerful shitheel got his feelings hurt. You ask me, people'd all be better off in places like this, interacting with other folks only when necessary."

"What about procreation?"

At this, the sobered Milton let out a hearty laugh.

"I said when necessary, Meller. And that ain't human. We all do that. We're just the only ones who've got to assign cosmic meaning to it. Spend enough time up here and you'll see. We assign cosmic meaning to all the wrong things and leave the best stuff of the world to rot unnoticed."

"You think I'm stupid, for wanting to go to the war."

"No, not stupid. I went too. Of my own volition."

"You volunteered?"

"Sure did."

"But you said you hated people."

"I did, but I saw what you see, felt what you felt. I wanted to make my mark."

"But you changed your mind."

"No. Just stopped trying. Realized that most things that are worthwhile aren't made by us. The marks we do leave, those are usually scars."

In the soft light of the single bulb, Leroy Milton did not look like a scarred man. He was middle aged, short in stature, with a full, black beard. His hair was sheared short, and he wore steel spectacles. He looked like just another man. It struck Samuel that he didn't look different somehow, changed in some physically irreparable way from what he had described. There was no mark upon him, and he had made no mark.

"What if I still feel the same? Guilty for being here and not there?"

"I'd be surprised if you didn't. Go on with it. Feel guilty. It's only natural. Only don't think you're missing out on some grand party."

Leroy Milton announced his intention to go to bed. He provided Samuel with some blankets that he used on the hard floor for a bed. It was only for one night. It was either that or up the seventy eight steps to the cot in the tower.

When Samuel woke in the morning, Leroy was boiling water on a hot plate for coffee.

"'Spose I don't have to tell you to be careful with this. Be a terrible thing for a fire lookout to start a fire. Still, a man needs coffee."

They sipped the grainy coffee (the beans had been crushed with the flat edge of a knife as best as he could) and looked out the windows, each of them sitting on the edge of the cot as there was nowhere else to sit. There was no residue of their talk from the night before, and they both took in the slow sunrise, already visible to those on the ground, as it summited the peaks like any old hiker and finally found its way into the sky to light the day.

"That's just about the most amazing thing I've ever seen."

"It gets better, young man. It happens every day."

4

With the departure of Milton, so did Samuel Meller's war years begin. Far away from the fighting in Europe, in Asia, and all the political intrigue that came with it. The significant events of the world were lost to him except in broad generalities. His own significant events were on a much smaller scale, but struck him all the same. There were nights when he was required to watch lightning strike all night, in case it might start fire. It often did, but most of those would burn out quickly, though he would dutifully report to ECC what happened. Some nights the moon shone so powerfully into his home that he would stay up all night reading one of his library books, or a book he could manage to wrangle from the village on his rare trips down. Natural moments were what marked his passage of time. He marked the sunset and sunrise each day, noting at what time each occurred, and this too was important. When rain lashed hard at the tower and he was certain he was swaying six feet in each direction as the tower lurched and lunged in the gale, he marked it in his memory. There was the moment when he made friends with an Elk. It stood at the bottom of the tower and looked up occasionally. Again and again, it would leave and come back, staring up at the tower as if waiting for Samuel to come down. When the lookout did manage the seventy eight steps down the tower to see the elk, the creature finally ran away, seeing that Samuel is not what he was looking up for, hoping for. On December seventh, 1941 there was a major fire. It was the most Samuel had ever spoken into his radio. They needed constant updates on the situation: which way the wind was blowing and from where, cloud cover percentage, what weather he had recently noticed. Anything at all he could tell them to help them manage the fire. For days, he hardly slept, staying always at the window, on his feet, tin coffee cup never far from hand, his microphone wet with spittle. This too, had begun with a lightning strike, but it did not burn out as Samuel had expected it might. No, it raged on with unexpected strength, blackening oaks, pines, and holly bushes alike. It was indiscriminate in its havoc, and even at four thousand feet, the air smelled of smoke. For weeks, the country had been in turmoil, in agony over the events of December seventh, and so was Samuel, only the reference point was quite different. It was an important day to the lookout, ignorant of world affairs though he was. Of course, on his next trip to the village, he found out that the war had come to America, even if it hadn't wanted it. He was surprised at his own reaction. He took it in like any other event, noted it in his logbook, and continued living. The Pearl Harbor Attack was nestled in Samuel's consciousness in between his most recent afternoon walk, and how he liked to hike all the way down to the river on bright days and dip his feet into the water. Though they were still miles away, he could sometimes hear the chatterings of the engineers and workers who were laying groundwork for a dam that Roosevelt wanted them to build. It seemed inconceivable even to Samuel, so removed from the world, that there could be enough men to build such a thing at a time like this.

These were the young lookout's thoughts while he dipped his feet in the cool, running water. They rolled over him just as the water did his toes. Not for any purpose other than that, simply to dip his feet did Samuel make the hike down. Samuel found that purpose was a malleable concept. He found that hiking ten miles and tiring his feet, just to put those feet into cool water was worth his time.

Each night, he sat on his cot, his back against the cool stones which made his home on top of the world, and wrote down the events of the day, inevitably beginning with a description of the sunrise, for the colors changed, and the sunset. Everything that happened in between took on a special resonance, when your days are filled with the human activity of only a single soul. The important aspects of a solitary life are often found outside of it, in the call of a bird of prey heard from on high, the floating mists rolling straight through the tower, leaving the windows with streaking raindrops going down, but no sound of rain, or the falling of a far away boulder, crashing crashing down the mountainside until it comes to rest.

There were small human accomplishments, and these he wrote of too: his whittling was greatly improving, and he had fashioned himself a corncob pipe that Eddard Morley would have been proud of. He hiked with consistency and vigor, keeping track of his travels as best he could. But as he sat on his cot, his pipe clenched between his teeth, the world he had left behind came back to him, flooded in on his senses and left him powerless. His world was one that was rapidly passing him by. The world he had left was two years gone, but was the same in his memory. There was nothing to change his idea of it. He had no news from home, though he wrote to both Amelia and his mother once a week, long letters that he worked on all week before his Sunday visit to the village and his PO box. For three years, this is how Samuel lived. He knew about major events in the real world, but nothing that could conceivably affect him. As far as he was concerned, his small town in Ohio had been motionless since his dramatic exit. One might think that such a feat of denial might be difficult, but it was not so hard for the young man. Young men, particularly those in the throes of both guilt and sadness, of regret and stubborn pride, those are the sorts who are most skilled at self-deception even under normal circumstances. And since Samuel had the continual advantage of living four thousand feet above the world, and wholly alone, there was no reality to intrude into his ever more absurd imaginings of his life back home. The further removed he became from his former life, the more his reference points drifted, until they were nothing of use, and he was doing nothing more than spinning yarns to an audience of one.

He walked about the woods those years and learned a great many things. He learned that moss growing only on the north side of a tree was a tall tale that ought to be extinguished. He learned the paralyzing fear of seeing a bear's eyes lock with your own. He learned to expand his knowledge of trees to include those most common in his new mountain home. He was arguably no longer an amateur naturalist, and certainly knew more than Thoreau who could rarely be bothered to leave his precious Northeast. Samuel learned what it was to be lost in the woods, having trail blazed too far and without enough food. On one occasion it took him three days to find his tower again. The forestry service had been on the verge of sending someone out to look for him.

"Thought you was on a bender," the normally-reticent ECC radio man said. I've been doing this long enough. Told them to wait it out a bit before wasting the resources."

In a way, the man from ECC was right. Samuel had been on a bender. He took to the woodsman's life with a fierceness that only a man with a deep hole inside him can. Fortunately for Samuel, in the long run it would meld to him in a positive way. There are few things that might actually come close to filling the hole in one's heart, and the woods are one such object.

Samuel learned the joy of experiencing the reality of one's death. Time and time again the mountains have a way of reminding those who brave them that human life is a precarious proposition in the best of times. One time in particular, Samuel felt as if he understood part of Milton's point about war. It was in the Summer of 1940, his second on the job, and a storm was approaching. That was obvious. The sun had long since set, but the sky was a fearsome reddish haze with cumulonimbus clouds gathering at a frenzied pace. There was no need for the sun in times like this. The storm was perfectly capable of keeping the sky lit as long as it so pleased. The skies opened up and the tower was berated with heavy drops and swayed in the wind. The tower swayed back and forth about six inches on a calm day. Samuel couldn't say how much it moved on stormy days, but it seemed at least thrice as much. Like a man in a rowboat on the ocean, Samuel clutched the railing of the tower, unable to say why he did not beat a retreat down the steps and into his cabin.

Something kept him rooted to the spot, staring out into the mouth of the devil. Lighting struck so nearby that its thunderous sound was simultaneous, yet Samuel remained in place. He had never been more frightened in his life. It was abundantly clear that the forces that shook the tower, that turned the river below to a roiling, black tempest, and which lit the sky without aid of the sun, these forces could snuff him without thought. He was smaller than the smallest sweetgum ball he crunched underneath his boots with occasional relish. Samuel looked at death and he did not win. He did not stare it down like some bullshit John Wayne cowboy, or northeastern gangster. Samuel looked at death and he blinked not once, but many times. He prostrated himself in the face of powers beyond that did not always show themselves, from which ordinary humans took great pains to hide. He learned the great gnostic folly of human existence, of the great game of make-believe that humans had endeavored to engage in for the last few centuries. If there were enough buildings, enough dams, enough destruction of our own making, wars and gangs and slavery, perhaps the real story would fade away. But Samuel could not look away from it anymore, and it was good.

The mountains were good to Samuel. Shuckstack Mountain assisted the young man in his learning, nudging its young pupil along, its visitor which lived on the most miniscule of peaks, straddling the great ranges of the Southeast. Samuel certainly grew in those early years, but at night, when the mountain was only the ground, its peaks hidden from view, and it was quiet, and the young man was perched on his corner bed, his back to the stone wall, his two kitchen pots hung on nails precariously above his head, he worked on his forever unreturned letters and failed to see his past with any clarity. So much men can learn, and yet not see what is most obvious.

It was not until 1942, the offseason, in the dead of winter, when the cabin beneath the tower was almost unbearably cold, the small stove and the fireplace never provided enough heat and the blankets never trapped the insufficient heat quite well enough, that he received a letter. There it was, sitting in his PO box like it was the most normal thing in the world. Three years and no incoming mail, yet there it was. Had the postal worker who placed it there marveled at its presence? Samuel certainly did. He slipped the letter into his flannel shirt pocket, tugged on his hat out of nervous habit, and went about his trip as if nothing was different. He purchased supplies that he needed, traded small talk with the few folks in town who he knew at all, though not well, and began his ascent back to the tower at midday. The roads through the mountains were new, put down by Roosevelt's men so that his others could do their work. Samuel did not like them, their strange, black asphalt, and was always pleased once he crossed the river, a weight releasing from him as he left man's world behind and returned to his more comfortable position as a visitor in the wild.

The letter weighed him down more than the bread, paper, and butter he had purchased. Insignificant though its weight might have been, it pulled his jacket and his body towards the earth as he determinedly moved upwards. The hike was no longer difficult for him, but these were different circumstances. When he made it back to the tower, still he put off the reading of the letter.

He did a midday check of the surrounding area and found nothing but mist. Next on his list was the roof. The weather on top of a mountain is more fierce than most people can imagine, and the tower had to take all of the pain. The roof needed some work, and it was Samuel's job to make sure the lookout remained in good shape. The letter he took from his pocket and placed it on the counter that held the radio and a few maps. Outside, braving the heights, tying a rope around his waist and to the tower steps, he mounted the roof of his perch. On top of the world, the wind in his face, at least forty one hundred feet above sea level, Samuel got to work laying pine tiles he had cut himself. The nails were paid for by the forest service, and the hammer came from the toolkit left behind by some long-gone man. With nails between his lips, Samuel softly laid out some pine straw as insulation, covered it with the tile, and nailed the tile in four corners. This he repeated again and again until the sun began to dip behind the far away peaks and the bluish tint of a mountain's early evening began.

His dinner he ate in silence, standing up at the windows as he always did, surveying the land, working. He rarely ate in his cabin, though all his cooking was done below. He preferred to work as he ate. Fire lookouts didn't have work hours. Work hours were all hours for Samuel. He was careful, making sure that an hour of daylight did not pass without him spending part of it on the search for telltale smoke. Even in the off-months when he was not being paid, and the service did not deem his eyes necessary, he kept watch. He felt a kinship with the forest that for him could not end when the rains came, could not be put away as in a drawer.

Finally, the sun long gone and near total dark having arrived, the night sounds just beginning their evening chorus, Samuel sat down to read his letter. It was from his mother, and it was dated from nearly a month earlier.

Samuel,
I have read your letters, though your father will not. I know he wants to desperately, but pride keeps him away. I could not bring myself to

respond up to this point, and for that I beg forgiveness. I admire the work that you are doing, and your father does too. Things here are much as they ever were, but completely different at the same time. Many of our boys are gone to war and the mood in town in rather down. They've just raised the draft age to thirty seven. Your father can hardly find a free man to help him around the farm and I fear he is working himself to death even with the small task of keeping our winter garden. All things considered, we get on well. We are lucky compared to some. It is with sadness that I tell you Del has passed on. Collapsed in his store one day last spring. Your father gave the eulogy at the service. Most folks found it to be very satisfactory. My mind wanders and I write to you of things you don't care about. You were never much for the town's gossip even when you were here. I will get to the short of it. Amelia Fribley is to be married. The man is named Ted and he's a military officer. He's set to be gone to North Africa any day, so they're getting married this very week. I know this must hurt you, but as your mother I thought you ought to know. I always liked her, but you've made your choice. Do consider coming home.

With love,

Your Mother.

So that was it then. She was already married. The letter had traveled for over a month. On some day when Samuel had been tallying cloud patterns or chopping wood, Amelia Fribley had been married. She had not once responded to a letter, but it had not stopped Samuel from writing them. He supposed that now there was no reason to keep writing. She had declared herself unwilling to wait, and thus had she acted. It was admirable, though hard for Samuel to acknowledge. She was the only girl he had ever really loved. Still, her marriage seemed far away. Still, his mind was in 1939 and was trapped there. That was the present in Ohio. His mother's letter was surreal, like a moving picture about sea monsters, having no relation to any objective reality. The world that felt so close to him at night, so near, that world held Amelia as she had been, his mother and father, Del, hell the whole of the midwest.

He read the letter again, tucked it back into its envelope and put it under his stack of books. No tears came to his eyes, and no immediate hurt arose, only the lingering feeling of irreality, of how small and childlike the world his mother described was. Even the south wood, though his mother had not mentioned it, must have changed. Perhaps not enough for any human eye to notice, but it had changed. What Samuel felt was not sadness, but a sense of perspective. For the first time in nearly three years, he was able to step away from the tower, to step back from his own obsession over the few years he and Amelia had shared together, and look around at the world as it was and see clearly. The irreality melted and left a cold, husk in its place. All this time, Samuel had put home away like a book in a bag, as if it were static, always ready to be picked up and read again at leisure. Samuel had left home in every sense, and only now, after this shot from the heavens, did he begin to think with any real seriousness about what might have happened to the people in his life since he had been in the tower.

It was unpleasant. The hurt came in. Sudden truths, put to paper and irrevocably etched into his memory were every bit as solid as the pine tiles he nailed into place forty one hundred feet above the world. It began to thunder on the mountain and Samuel let the pain come. No rain fell, but thunder and wind shook the tower. It was structurally sound, though early nights in the tower just after the departure of Leroy Milton, Samuel had feared as the tower swayed. He knew now that all was okay. Roosevelt's smart engineers had designed it that way. It was supposed to sway, but it was always okay. Just fine.

The thunder raged and Samuel came to terms with life as best he could. Amelia Fribley had never planned on waiting for him. She had told him so to his face. He simply hadn't believed it. She may have loved him once, but now she was married to someone else. People were fighting, and they were dying. The world was in turmoil. The guilt returned and he remembered Leroy Milton's words. He let it wash over him and he accepted it. Lighting rang out in the night, lighting up the solitary lookout in the sky. Samuel had been cruel to his father, to his mother, so much so that she had struggled to write to him though she missed him. He had taunted them with his blase letters, pretending as if life had not irrevocably changed, as if he had not walked out on them in a blaze of angst and indecision.

It hurt, but it was worth it. All this time, he had stood in his tower and surveyed thousands of miles, and yet he had seen nothing of himself. A solitary man, cloistered from the world and all of its problems, writing callous letters devoid of social or cultural context. Wind caused the tower to sway and the cot slid away from the wall. Wolves howled as they often did, their dirges a blow struck across Samuel's body. He could see now what a fool he had been, what stunning lack of imagination had been on display on his part. At the root of it all: denial. He let it all go and accepted the world for what it was. He fell asleep in the middle of the night in the tower cot, exhausted with his own effort of self discovery.

5

Samuel awoke with the sun, as he always did up there with no way to hide from it, and he found a bright new dawn. He was not in the same place he had been the morning previous. The revelations of the night before had not left him. They stayed. They marked him. But the blue ridges were no less beautiful to him, the river far below no less reflective of the trees thousands of feet above its surface, and the smell of his hand-crushed coffee beans no less soothing. In fact, they were better than they had been before. What had once acted as a salve on an unseen wound, now made deposits in an equally unseen column. Samuel saw his post more clearly than he ever had before in his nearly three years in the tower, and he had his mother and Amelia Fribley to thank. To his mother, he jotted a short reply, his coffee cup resting next to his roughly hewn paper.

Mother,
I love hearing from you. Please write again. All is well on the tower. I am sure the men from town will represent us well in the war. Tell

father I say hello, even if he cares not to answer. Please send along my congratulations to Amelia and Ted. I'm sure they will be very happy.

It was all he could manage. He hoped to write more to his mother later, but for the time being, he put his letter down, pleased with the effort. It was another day on the mountain and there was work to be done. There were peaks and valleys which had been obscured by fog for days that needed to be observed if possible, there was always a need for more stovewood, and the roof was not yet finished. Life on the mountain marched on, leaving little time for grief. Self-reflection was for nighttime in the glass box. Daytime was for action and self-care of a more practical kind.

As he went about his duties, Samuel continued to marvel at how changed he felt, as if a very literal weight had departed from his chest. He had been carrying around the weight of three years on his chest, the news of the real world piling on higher and higher as he refused to acknowledge its existence. But now, its weight lifted, its presence the last years was even further highlighted. The ax he used for chopping was lighter, the roofing nails went into the pine tiles like butter, and the clouds moved away from his recently hidden peaks as if blown by a puff of air from his very mouth. It was a part of the beauty of the glass box on the top of the world, any dereliction of duty would lead to a great deal of personal discomfort. Days passed, weeks, and Samuel came to a new appreciation for his routine, the beauty of it, the simplicity. It shaped the tenor of his days and his moods, an adze through well-worked wood. Samuel found it better to be sad than to be forever on the brink. His newfound acceptance of what had happened in his life filled him with sadness yes, and at times, walking through the steep woods, fog in his eyes, or standing at the windows of his box, keeping his watch, he broke down and cried. But it was a tangible outpouring of emotion, and that seemed appropriate. His bedtime farce of writing to Amelia now struck him for what it had always been: a boy's foolishness while playing at a man's life. It was hard to explain the happiness of his first man's grief, and there was no one around to spin his wheels with, so

Samuel did what was right in front of him, which is all that anyone can be expected to do with any kind of aplomb.

Three weeks past his mother's letter, Samuel was making his way down the mountain to the village. He had not yet finished his letter, but the mere spectre of the letter had kept him from going to town, and now he was in desperate need. He was out of lightbulbs and had been calling it a night as soon as the sun went down behind the peaks, and his food supply was quite low. He could no longer put off the trip to town. He brought a pocket notebook with a leather tie strap. It was his identification book. He had been doing his best to identify as many species of plants in his new terrain ever since he had arrived. Samuel had always imagined himself as a naturalist back home, but he had been aided by being the son of a farmer, and having access to a whole swath of land. He had foolishly imagined that his knowledge of flora was sufficient. It was of course, not shabby for the midwest, but the mountains of the american southeast were a whole different animal and Samuel was but a mere schoolboy in the hands of mother nature once more. His trips to town were always begun early in the morning so that there was no rush.

He stopped periodically at the base of a tree he was unfamiliar with, picked up a leaf or two, and began to flip through his field guide. It was not a part of Samuel's job to be familiar with all of the species of tree that grew within his views, but it struck him personally as within the realm of his duties, and he set to it with vigor. At the base of the tree he stood, craning his neck up to get a look at the height, walked around to estimate the trunk, and picked up a few more leaves to make sure they were consistent with what he thought. Once Samuel was certain, he sat down with his back against the stippled trunk, and opened his journal, untying the leather band. He stopped for a moment, pondering over how he would name the tree. His notebook was full of notations such as "Raccoon's Nest Loblolly Pine" and "MT hearts LR Dogwood," always taking the time to denote them thus so that he would not forget them. With the tripartite leaves sitting in his lap, the notebook resting just on top of them, he wrote "Three Week Grief, Water Oak." He took the time to note it was a member of the red oak family, and had small, bitter acorns before sliding one one of the leaves into the book, closing it back up, and tying the leather cord once more. Standing up, he made his way down the mountain towards the village.

There were no comments in reference to how long he had been gone. Despite his relative status as a member of the community, whoever held the post of fire lookout at Shuckstack Tower was always a bit of a mystery to the folks in the village. They whispered among themselves about what kind of man could live way up there, exposed to the world, all alone, for such long periods of time.

> "Must be some kind of crazy if you ask me."
> "Shouldn't he be with the other boys, taking fire from the Nazis?"
> "Heard he's too deaf for the army."

"No it's too blind. Seen his glasses? Thicker than a two by four they are."

"Does a good job doesn't he? Leave him be."

"How should we know he's doing a good job?"

"Ain't burned down have we? That's his job."

"I heard he sends letters but never gets any."

"What business of yours is that?"

"Do you think he's a queer?"

"That much time alone could have any kind of effect on a man."

"Heard the last man up there jumped. That's why it was empty for awhile."

"He just got too old. That's why they brought in someone so young."

"It's a last line of defense against the Nazis. There's a gun turret up there to mow them down if they ever make it to the valley."

Samuel knew that he was whispered about, but as he had come from a small town, he held nothing against the people, and nor could he blame them for being suspicious of someone willing to spend nearly all of his time alone on the top of a mountain. It was their right to think of him as some kind of cheap dime mystery.

His rucksack nearly full with amenities he had put off purchasing for too long, Samuel reflexively made his way to the post office. He had nothing to send, and did not expect there to be anything else for him, but it was a part of his routine. He fit his key into the lock and turned, and once again, twice in two visits, there was a letter in his box. The young fire lookout stared at the letter, alone in the post office that morning. Here he was, having spent the better part of three weeks coming to terms with his life, having had it laid bare before him by a letter full of truths he had refused to acknowledge, and now there was another one. He gave legitimate thought to leaving the letter, to putting it off in case it might throw him off in some way, ruin the inner peace he had achieved, if only for a moment in the scope of his life. In the end, Samuel pocketed the letter, closed his PO box, and began the trek back to the glass box. It had been his intention to stop and identify another tree on his way back up the mountain, if for no other reason than to give his aching shoulders a break from the cutting straps of his rucksack, filled to the bursting due to his own sloth. Samuel did not stop and the notebook stayed in his back pocket, the letter folded between its pages, poisoning the whole enterprise. He had not even deigned to look at who it was from. It did not matter. Letters were an intrusion on his neatly ordered life, and he was not going to deal with it at this point in time.

Unfortunately, upon his return to the tower, Samuel realized that he had been entirely too efficient in the last few weeks, and had little to do to occupy his mind. The wood pile was stacked high, the roof had been finished, and the perimeter of the tower had been scoured at the base for any signs of deterioration. The horizon was clean, not even the near-constant cloud and fog cover present to give him pause. The mountains were calm and blue in the early afternoon. Books did not hold his attention, the words sliding in front of his eyes without meaning, not reaching his brain, resulting in Samuel re-reading the same page again and again. Finally, he decided to pick points on the horizon and calculate their coordinates. There was nothing wrong with adding new points of reference to the windows of the glass box. Samuel spent the hours of the afternoon waiting for the sun to go down, staring southeast towards the blue ridge, the occasional wheeling red tail hawk the only distraction from his feverish calculations. If there was a fire in the blue ridge, there would be no doubt in what quadrant it lay. Samuel would be able to relay the information so quickly, the ECC operator's head would spin.

When the sun went down, Samuel was mentally exhausted, having frayed his nerves to the nib, and gratefully took the refuge of his cot without dinner, brushing his teeth, or replacing the lightbulb. He slept the sleep of the dead, though he would not sleep for long. It isn't considered a positive development to wake up to the smell of smoke under any circumstances, but to Samuel Meller, the young fire lookout atop Shuckstack Tower, straddling the blue ridge, the smokies, and more it was the worst possible way to come to consciousness. In the darkness, he stumbled about the small room at the roof of the world, trying to find his light bulb so that he could screw it in, only so that he could then find his clothes, a rope, and the courage to venture up the seventy eight steps and into the box in the middle of the night to turn on the spotlight. All of these things Samuel did somewhat mechanically, still under the spell of sleep, not recognizing the danger of his actions. He could feel the beating of his heart against his ribcage, struggling to escape. His glasses fogging with his heavy breathing, Samuel stood at his desk in the sky and began to go through the motions of his job, taking measurements as best he could as the circling spotlight made its way around again and again, lighting up the night in the mountains for brief glimpses only. The fire was not far off at all, less than two miles by Samuel's calculations, down in the valley too near the river Samuel walked to in order to dip his toes. Once his calculations finished, they were as tight as he could manage, which was better than usual considering the relative closeness of the blaze. On the radio, the ECC operator was sleepy, but jolted awake the by unusually harsh tone from the usually soft spoken Shuckstack lookout.

"You'll," the operator stumbled. "You'll have to get down there and help fight the blaze. You'll be first on the scene. Do you know your first line of order?"

"Yes," he responded mechanically. "I do."

"Be safe, lookout."

Samuel pulled on his boots, going over the protocol in his head. So many days after Milton had left spent poring over the protocol, Milton's script in the margins, making jokes, offering suggestions that were written for only Samuel's eyes. He had enjoyed them while reading through, but now they were of life and death importance. At the bottom of the tower, Samuel retrieved his axe from under the tarp protecting both it and the woodpile. He set up a small log on his chopping stump and let the axe fall into it, swinging it up and down a few times to make sure the log was well attached. With the flashing light of the tower leading his difficult way, his axe slung over his shoulder, flannel jacket pulled tight against the night, an extra around his waist to block the smoke, he began his descent into the valley.

It was slow-going, careful work. Samuel would be no good to anyone if he got himself killed on his way down, and the light provided by the tower was less and less helpful the deeper into the valley he traveled. The moon was a dull, waning gibbous, headed to crescent in a day's time and provided little in the way of light. By the time Samuel was close enough to see the fire, he had long since tied his second shirt around his face. His hot, muffled breath came in short rasps, his heart beating rapidly. His position staked out, Samuel began to build a perimeter a best he could. His job was to start the job that many men would have to continue. He raised his axe, the log attached, down into the dirt, again and again, using it as a trench digging tool. Samuel was miniscule in the sight of trees, but less than such in the sight of a blazing fire, making shadows of the trees as the flames that licked at others made shadows of the rest of the world, shapes floating listlessly by the man silently at work, lifting the ax over his head with precision, letting the weight of the head and the piece of wood do all the work. The ground was hard, full of roots, and generally opposed to all of Samuel's efforts. Still, he soldiered on, banking fatigue like he never had before, nothing but will keeping him standing, moving, working. He was so engrossed in his work that he had to be notified when the firefighters arrived. Had he been pressed to it, Samuel would not have been able to say how long he had been working. They put their hands on his shoulders and stopped him physically, pulling his shirt down from his face to reveal his sooty visage, his eyes reddened badly.

"You need to get some help," one of them said. "We'll take it from here. You've done your job."

The words were only the movements of the man's lips to Samuel. He realized in that moment that he could not hear. He could not recall the last thing he had heard. Was it the Shumard oak, *quercus shumardii,* massive and elusive red oak of the forest bursting from the inside, its six foot wide trunk opening up like the gates of hell? The axe, the wood thrown off, colliding with a submerged boulder, shooting sparks high into the sky? He did not know, but allowed himself to be lead away, and it was those few footsteps that he remembered. Past there it was only darkness.

He collapsed to the ground from equal parts exhaustion, smoke inhalation, and stress. When Samuel awoke, he was still on the ground, but his head was clearer, and a familiar face hovered above him.

"Happy to see me? Not thrilled myself. Long hike you know. You were really out though. Drink this."

Milton thrust a skin of water into Samuel's hands and commanded the still-dazed lookout to drink. After another twenty minutes of steadily intaking water, Samuel was able to sit up, and by the time the sun was high in the sky, the afternoon after Samuel had been awoken in the night, he and Milton began the hike back to Shuckstack tower.

"Not that I'm thrilled to be your babysitter once more. Good job though. We'll ten am that fire tomorrow."

"Thanks," Samuel said quietly.

It was the policy of the forest service to put out any fire by ten am the morning after it had been reported. If it wasn't contained by then...ten am the next morning was the new target. This continued indefinitely until the blaze was contained. Samuel had done his part.

"You'd dug out a hell of a lot of a perimeter for one man. That log trick with this," Milton said, indicating the axe that he carried over his own shoulder, "that was damn clever. You should mark that down in the log."

Samuel was understandably sore, and still tired. He did not much feel like chatting with Milton on their trek back to Shuckstack. Once they reached the tower, Samuel went immediately to the windows up high, and Milton busied himself with getting a dinner together in the cabin that had once been his. It had been a long time since either of them had eaten a proper meal.

"Your rainwater tank, keep it locked?"

Samuel pointed to the hook on the wall by the door as his answer.

"Never much saw the point myself," Milton said. "Be back shortly. We'll get something going."

While Milton bothered himself about getting food and tea ready for them, Samuel continued to stare out the window at the steadily rising smoke. At first, smoke was always a pure white, twisting and whirling about in the high altitude winds, but once it had chewed up enough undergrowth grass and reached the thick pine groves it took on a darker, more ominous color.

"Not doing yourself any good to stare at it. You've been lucky thus far. First one you've had to get your hands dirty for."

"It's still burning."

"Sometimes it's just got to burn. Natives used to set the forest on fire on purpose. Some that say we're fools for not letting 'em go sometimes."

"Ten am," Samuel said, repeating the company line.

"Aye, ten am. You did good, son."

Milton put a hand on Samuel's shoulder and spun him around. "Now eat. It's not a request."

Samuel felt immeasurably better after drinking more water and eating the canned soup that Milton had heated in the wood stove. The two men stayed up by the light of the fire and traded stories of how they had been for the last two years. Milton only stayed in his tower during the on season, choosing to tend bar during the six months when his presence wasn't strictly necessary in the tower.

"Maybe you ought to think about taking some time, Meller. You've been up here a long time."

"I go to the village from time to time. I get mail," he added quietly, nodding towards the desk at the window.

"Well you're out of your mind if you ask me, and I'm one of the initiated.'

"At first, I was hiding. You'd be right about me. I was out of my mind. I was hiding from my own poor decisions, unable to go home and face what I'd done, but that's not it anymore. I love it here. This place is unsullied, and I don't mean because of the trees or the peaks or anything like what Thoreau meant. It's unsullied for me. What I've gone through up here, all of the pain and struggle, along with the grinding day to day battle to keep myself a person in the absence of other peoples to bounce my personhood off of, it's been pure. All my troubles back home, the ones I caused and otherwise, they're all nothing up here. Up here, the only problems that matter are the biggest problems there are."

"At some point, you've got to leave the mountain."

"Maybe."

"Our lives have a way of intruding in on us, even up here."

Samuel thought of the unopened letter, sitting by the window in the tower as the smoke curled up high into the sky, flouting all of his best human effort that had so exhausted him. He thought of the letter, still unopened, unknown and crumpling in the ashes of the Shumard oak he had witnessed burst from the inside in a ball of fire.

"For now," Samuel said. "It's home for me."

Milton kept a closer tab on the outside world than Samuel. He was surprised to learn that Samuel rarely even listened to the news or to baseball games. He was able to tell the younger man about the war effort, about how things didn't look so good, and how Hitler was making good on his promises.

"Man like that, hard to square with."

"I get it," Samuel said.

"How do you mean?"

"Obviously he's a new low, but doesn't he seem to you to be the obvious continuation of our man-made evolution? Men like him, they aren't made in a vacuum. He's the order of things. And now we're horrified at what we've done, and all these boys my age have to die."

"Is that it?" Milton asked. "You want to die. That why you nearly killed yourself out there? I told you to feel your guilt, but not to give into it."

"No, that's not it. At least not entirely. I did what I always would have done. Just how I feel about it now is colored by the war."

"It's why you avoid hearing about it."

"That's about the shape of it. You know I always wanted to be important? I spent my childhood wanting to be remembered, to do something in my life that would change the world."

"Now, I told you the war ain't all that."

"That's not what I mean. I mean I wasn't just wrong about that, I was wrong about the goal. Why bother being important? Happiest I've ever been in my life was loving a woman. That doesn't make me unique, or important. It makes me alive, and I couldn't see it for what it was, what I had and threw away. She always did. She was always smarter than me."

"Ain't that always the way."

"Milton, would you like a bit of bourbon?"

"Young man, that's the most sense you've spoken all night."

Samuel grinned at his visitor, happy for the moment in sharing his space once again, if only for a short while. The world was never too much with Milton. He was a man who understood the pull of the tower. For this reason, Samuel was sad to see his friend go in the morning. It was difficult to place the crux of his feelings for Milton, as the two men had hardly spent two days together in as many years, and yet he felt like an old friend already. He watched the older lookout until he disappeared from the tower's view, leaving Samuel once again alone on top of the world, though this time two years later, much more prepared than he had been at last parting.

6

For days, things were much as they had been before the fire in the valley had started. It took three more ten am's in order for the crew of men to fully contain the Valley Letter Fire, as it was entered into the logbook. It was the lookout's job to name the fire, and it was not the first fire in the valley for the season, though it was the first major event. To distinguish it, Samuel named it Valley Letter. It was one of the few creative aspects of his job. Despite his somewhat public acknowledgement of the existence of the letter, he still had not read it, or even flipped it over to see who it was from. It took weeks for Samuel to do that, and by the time he did, he wished he had done it much earlier and had not been such a coward.

Samuel,

Forgive the delay in my reply, but I think you will agree that sometimes in the course of things, an extended absence as they say "makes the heart grow fonder." I find this is the case with our friendship, which seems appropriate to how ours began in such a short period. It seems strange to me now that you are a man in full standing these days, but also fills me with something akin to a father's pride if you'll allow it. If I am to understand correctly, this will reach you somewhere in the smoky mountains where you are serving as a lookout. You always did have an affinity for nature, and I think such a position suits you just fine. For myself, there is little worthy of what might be called news, or be of interest to you, but I will do my best to summarize. I find myself with enough money saved to enter something like retirement now at my advanced age. Should I live past the money I have saved, I shall count myself fortunate, though it seems unlikely. With time on my hands for the first since I was a young man of your approximate age, I wonder what to do with myself. I have spent much of the last days walking about Baltimore (that is where I am living now, if you did not know) and wondering what the purpose of a man is, if he cannot perform any kind of work that's good for something. This must be why I've never understood the suited men and their jobs that are composed of playing at invisible money. A thought has recently struck me is this: why should I not visit young Samuel Meller? The mystique of the high mountains and the crisp air has admittedly gotten ahold of this old man. What do you say to this old man? Will you have me for a short while? I'll await your reply.

Your friend,
Eddard Morley

Samuel engaged in hours of mental self flagellation before he could even begin to formulate a response worthy of paper. He had in fact never finished his response to his mother, but he was determined to respond to this missive. He could hardly think of something more wonderful than a visit from Eddard. Eddard, even before Amelia, had been the first person who had called out Samuel's bullshit for what it was. He understood Samuel well enough almost immediately so that he could cut him to the core. In a way that his father had never been able to, Eddard had forced Samuel to confront his flaws head-on in the mirror. It now seemed likely to the young lookout that had Eddard and the vagrants been living in the old barn on the night it had burned down, Samuel never would have run away. Eddard would have convinced him of the stupidity of his rash actions and Samuel would have been married to Amelia instead of a mountain. The mountain was a good spouse, loyal, strong, and immovable, but it was not

Amelia. When he had composed himself enough to write a letter, it was brief, but good enough in his estimation. In a small amount of words, there were less opportunities for foolishness.

> *Eddard,*
> *Set out for Bryson City as soon as you receive this reply. At the Forest Service office there they can lead you to me. It would be my honor to host you.*
> *Your friend,*
> *Samuel*

He departed for the village that very afternoon to post his letter as soon as possible, stopping only on his descent to mark a species of birch that had no business in his spot in the world. He was quite certain that the tree in question was a paper birch, prized by ancient peoples for the building of canoes and cradles, but native to only the most northerly patches of the United States and Canada. Early adventurers must have inadvertently brought the species to the smokies, and here was the evidence, hundreds of years on. The romance of it thrilled Samuel, this tree being evidence of the exploits and explorations of men from thousands of miles to his north into his own sacred territory. It occupied his mind much of the way to the village and back, perhaps saving him too much self-thought about his long delay in answering the letter from Eddard. On his return trip home, he even peeled a bit of the bark to take back to the tower, and which he tacked the wall just above his cabin sink, right below the window line, a constant reminder that though he could see for hundreds of miles at night and see no human light, he was far from alone. He communed with great men of the past, and with the great silent sentinels of the earth.

On the morning of Eddard's arrival, Samuel woke in a good mood, though there was no way to know what good the day held in store. He sipped his coffee upright as he always did, his staring posture out the window in vain, as cloud cover was complete and total. It was not so much raining as the air was mostly composed of water. Rainfall requires being far enough below the creation of the water for it to fall. Samuel was always grateful for rainy days, as it prevented him from his least favorite duty of his watch. At the bottom of the tower, a quarter mile away, hanging from a tree branch was two bundles of cloth: one which Samuel dipped in water every late afternoon, the other he left dry. The relative difference between the two was how humidity was measured on the mountain. When it was raining, he could log one hundred percent humidity calmly in his book and move on to the next thing. Cloud cover, one hundred percent. There was no need to have the radio volume turned up in order to hear dispatch tell him there was little chance of fire. Any man could see. Samuel also enjoyed rainy mornings for the cloistered feeling it gave him. Far from being claustrophobic, Samuel loved the feeling of being unable to see more than a hundred yards in any direction, alone in his tower like a private study room in an abnormally quiet library. It was the most peaceful kind of day on the lookout. The views of a clear day, making out the shadows of lives of animals that had called the peaks of hundreds of miles away home for thousands of years, the sheer scope of attempting to count the number of trees in even a tiny portion of the horizon, it was stunning in its beauty, but also overwhelming. On clear days, Samuel liked to go on hikes, have his feet on the ground, to look up and see each tree in its individual detail, only to return to the tower once his head was screwed back on properly.

The day of Eddard Morley's arrival was one of those near-perfect days when Samuel chose one of his most worn books, read so many times that he could pick a page at random and begin, and stood in front of the blank canvas of cloud cover, reading until he was too tired to stand anymore. Then, a lazy afternoon nap, then the careful cultivation of a pot of chili over the course of several hours, adding spices, testing the taste, repeating, for hours until he finally dined late in the night, happy in front of his fire with his perfect chili, slightly different perfection each time, and his book like an intellectual blanket.

By mid-morning when he first heard something out of the ordinary, Samuel was already thinking about his rainy-day chili. What he heard was a halloo. On a day like this, the only thing to do was to decamp, make his way down the steps. There was the occasional hiker, looking for a moment's rest, a man to bare his troubles to for an hour or so, and Samuel was unfailingly kind to his fellow nature lovers. He felt sometimes pangs of envy for their daily ramblings, their constant movement, and they too likely imagined his cloistered existence superior to their wanderings.

The possibility that it might be Eddard did not cross Samuel's mind until the old man himself was well within view. It had been just over a month since he had posted his letter, and here the man was. He was older certainly, and thinner, his beard clinging to a face sunken with age. But he was the same man. Samuel embraced him, pleased beyond measure to see his old friend after so many years. Eddard felt small in the young lookout's embrace, like a child, but his voice was just the same.

"Samuel."

"Eddard."

"I barely made it. Had to stop a dozen times. You live a bit out of the way."

"Did you imagine I lived at the top of a mountain in some abstract way, but not in reality?"

"Something like that, I think. Still, I'm glad as hell to see you."

"I feel the same. We've a lot to talk about, and plenty of time to do it. Let me carry your pack. We've got seventy eight steps to go yet, assuming you came all this way to see the view."

"You'll do no such thing," he said, swinging his pack over his back.

Samuel threw up his arms and relented to his friend, though he could not help but worry. The old man looked so frail these days, far from the hearty man who had helped his father keep the old barn upright with massive joists.

"So," Eddard said once they were settled in, a kettle of water boiling for more coffee, his pipe lit properly and filling the small space with aromatic smoke of his prized cherry tobacco. "Let's hear it."

"Hear what?"

"Don't insult me, boy. No married man lives in a box on top of the mountain for years at a time."

"Mountains make decent spouses at times."

"Poor metaphor to hide behind if you ask me. Come now, you do me a disservice."

"I left."

7

For the next several hours, Eddard listened to the pained ramblings of his young friend. He listened as Samuel explained his first flight from home to Cleveland, his disappointment that no army was going to take him, and his decision to not go home even then. He told Eddard of the conscientious objectors who served the country by manning dangerous fire crews, what his job entailed, his early days in the tower, and even his own self-realization of his stupidity. He laid his soul bare for the old man, and tried to explain the partial peace he had reached with life from the mountaintop.

"Sounds as if you've reckoned with your choices."

"Took some time. Lost a fine woman."

"Fine person from what I remember. Not just woman. Smarter'n you. That's for sure."

"She always got it."

"Didn't need the top of the world to find any truths did she? No, that seems to be peculiarly a man's issue. Sometimes we need deprivation and to live out the most abject consequences of our decisions until we can be made to see what was always right in front of our faces."

"And here we are."

"Here we are," Eddard said. "I'm sorry, Samuel. I'm sorry about her. I'm sure you're hurting."

"I took comfort in you, somewhat. Do you remember telling me about your wife?"

"Aye."

"You were so calm, so understanding of the situation. I thought of that when I was hurting the most. It helped."

"The truth," Eddard said. "Is that you were a boy."

"What's that mean?"

"It means that now you're a man and I'll tell you. I wasn't calm, and I wasn't reasonable. I was in more pain than I've been in my whole life that year in your father's barn. Wanted to die most days thinking of her with someone else, thinking on how I failed to support her when I vowed to do just that. I was hurting so much,

Samuel. Too much to tell a boy. Wouldn't have been right."

"I never knew."

"Of course you didn't. I was the mystical old man to you. You young people think age is so mysterious. Still, we both needed a friend didn't we?"

"We did."

Samuel had never considered the truth of his friend's words before. He had held Eddard in a kind of superhuman light, and in some sense still did. He had always been so far ahead of Samuel in life that he was untouchable. Samuel had done him a disservice in not imagining his friend as a full being, a being hurt and a being whom he couldn't ever fully understand, like anybody else.

"I'm sorry, Eddard."

"You've nothing to be sorry for. If I'd wanted sympathy, asking it from a boy would've been a fool thing to do. You helped me too. I was able to get outside of myself for the first time with you. Helping you with Amelia was a joy for me, allowed me to live through your youth, that first moment of love. I'd not change it."

"Couple of blubberers aren't we?"
"Seems that way."
"Whiskey?"
"Atta boy."

That was how Eddard's visit went at first. The two men would spend time reminiscing, comforting each other in the decisions that had been made over the years, each of them, as any man does, with plenty to regret and with a sympathetic ear to hear to it. Their time together went in patterns: a bout of shared misery, followed by laughing at themselves and their blubbering, and then a time of cleansing in which Samuel would lead Eddard on short hiking loops around his favorite places. Eddard was weak in his old age, and could not hike far, but Samuel was patient. Stopping often to let the old man catch his breath, narrating the hikes with tales of what animals he had seen near there, or giving the latin names of the trees their were passing by: quercus nigra, pinus taeda, cornus florida: black bear and cubs, a red fox with a raccoon in its mouth loping along, a wild boar, hissing and snorting.

"And you better hope we don't see one of those, because I'll be leaving you behind old man."

"You'll run from a pig?"

"This is no pig, Eddard. It's a wild, mountain boar. These creatures have survived for thousands of years. We brought them here and they've taken the landscape by the balls and won't let go. There's free reign on hunting them, but I'd sooner hunt bear or bobcat. They'll charge at you. No fear. Gore you with their tusks. Ancient kings are said to have died hunting them with spears."

"Sounds like a good way to fuck up a lineage."

"Exactly. And I'd like to leave mine intact for the moment."

It concerned Samuel how tired Eddard got from walking only a short while, but he could not say what Eddard Morley's age was exactly, and he didn't care to ask. It must have taken the old man hours and hours to make the hike up the mountain. It seemed obvious to Samuel that he would have to escort the old man whenever he chose to leave, and he planned to make his trip the village align with Eddard's departure. In the meantime, Samuel was in no rush to ask the old man when exactly he was planning to leave. For all the time he had spent alone, he found himself enjoying the company.

They were kind days, the days of Eddard's visit. Though the two men had never spent so much time together, they like the soldiers so far away, found in each other a camaraderie neither knew was possible for themselves. It was a time that would live on in Samuel's memory for the entirety of his days. Unlike the men in the service, the men who could see well enough to die, they were not memories that would tear him down, but ones that reminded him why life was worth living. For his whole life, snatches of conversation from those fine days floated into Samuel's wandering brain, whether he was sitting in a rocking chair, smoking sweet tobacco, reading a book in bed, or walking in the woods. The words came back and he did not allow them to bring him low.

...

"Called a 'smoke' when we spot a fire. Got to radio it in with all the particulars. Windspeed, humidity, all the rest, and where the smoke is of course."

"And you get to name them?"

"Sure do."

"Seems like a hell of a responsibility for someone who gets paid next to nothing. Ever think of naming one witch's tit, so they've got to say that on the radio?"

"Witch's tit is blazing at an acre a minute."

"Perimeter being dug around witch's tit."

"Witch's tit ought to burn out by the time it hits the creek. Trout may die by tit's wrath."

...

"Seems like a fool thing to me."

"Why? It's my whole calling up here."

"Well, how long has this tower been here?"

"Shuckstack's been here about fifteen years, but some others for much longer."

"Not as long as these forests have been here."

"Obviously."

"If the forests needed some smartass in a tower to protect it from fire, then why have they existed for millions of years?"

"I don't know, Eddard. I think that question might be above my paygrade. My instructions say that I spot, and they try to put it out by ten am. If not this day, then the next."

"Man's foolishness if you ask me."

"You know, I don't think I did."

...

"Your father."

"My father is the best man you've ever met? It was a serious question. A man gets to thinking on serious things up here, and now you're making fun of me."

"I'm doing no such thing. You've never had a proper appreciation for your old man. I've never thought it was right."

"He's a farmer."

"You're a pair of eyes. You only think you're better because the views are nice. Farmer, banker, railway man. I don't give a shit what he is, but he was always a damn fine person."

"Can we talk about something else?"

...

"Are you going to make another move?"

"I'm thinking."

"You've been thinking for an hour. At some point it's not chess anymore, it's just two people sitting on the ground."

"I can't remember which piece is which. The pine cone is the rook?"

"No, the bark is the rook. The pine cone is the knight."

"I thought the acorn was the knight."

"The acorns are pawns. How many knights did you think you have?"

"Was never much for chess."

...

"It's beautiful. Like a whole different part of the world then the morning I arrived."

"Sometimes it'll look different every morning for a week."

"Can I use the radio?"

"No."

Into the radio:

"Sky's prettier than an expensive whore with a handprint on her ass. About as red as one too."

"Shuckstack, is that you?"

"Goddammit, Eddard."

"Just thought they ought to know way down there."

...

"You need some help with that?"

"I think I know how to tamp my own pipe."

"Well you're spilling all over the floor."

"You not going to have time to clean it up?"

...

"We never did, no. We were waiting until we got married."

"That's a hell of a thing."

"What I miss most is her telling me off. I know it sounds loony, but it's true."

"You want some help? I've got some thoughts I could share."

"You're not nearly pretty enough."

"That's god's truth if I've ever heard it."

"I don't believe in God."

"Man should believe in something. Keeps him honest."

"I believe in plenty of things. Just not god."

"Young man's thoughts."

"Maybe God is just the result of an old man's thoughts. Closer you get to death, more you're looking for a reason to believe."

"I'd rather you were wrong."

"I think most people would. Hence God."

...

8

Sometimes they went hours without speaking at all, spending time in amiable silence, communing with each other and with the mountain. Shuckstack spoke to the old man as much as the young. It was quite a place to arrive at after running away from your problems. Fortuitous.
It was during one of these periods of silence that Samuel asked Eddard how long he was planning on staying.

"Not that I'm rushing you out the door or anything."

"I figured you'd ask that eventually."

"Seems like an obvious line of thinking."

"If I'm telling the truth, I've been putting something off I ought to have told you when I arrived."

"What's that?"

The old man puffed at his pipe, doing his best imitation of the White Pine fire in the blue ridge, seventeen acres and counting, puffs of smoke rising periodically.

"I'm not well."

"Anyone can see that."

"I'm dying, Samuel."

Samuel could not have said that he expected his friend to utter these words, but surprise nor was he captured by a sense of surprise. The thought had been allowed to huddle somewhere in the recesses of his consciousness, never fully acknowledged, but not shown the door either.

"You never intended on going back down the mountain."

It wasn't posed as a question, because Samuel knew it wasn't one.

"They say it's like drowning, only slower. I lived a hard life, Samuel."

"Why didn't you tell me?"

Eddard was crying, and Samuel could not bring himself to look him in the eye any longer. Here was a frail, old man brought low by life. There was nothing hidden any longer.

"I'm afraid. I've got no one. Don't you think I feel guilty at the burden I'm putting on you? Just a boy I knew once, and I come to you with a request like this. I know it's not fair, but you're the closest thing I've got to kin, as sad as that is, it's the truth."

"How long?"

"Months maybe. They don't know really. It's no exact science."

"So you want me to watch you die?"

"No, I don't. That's the part I've been putting off. I don't want to drown, Samuel. I've stolen some morphine, God forgive me. When it gets bad…"

This had not crossed Samuel's mind, either in concrete or vaporous form. He had not expected his friend to ask him something like that. Revulsion as his immediate reaction.

"No. I won't do it. You can't ask me that."

"I'm afraid of drowning. Never been able to swim, Samuel, not for my whole life. And now they tell me I'm going to go under, not be able to breathe, pulling it through a straw in the reeds like a bandit. Please, Samuel."

"And then what? You're gone. But I have to stay. I have to live. Don't you see that?"

"I do. It's a terrible thing to ask, and I'd ask just about anyone else if I could. These have been just about the finest weeks of my life up here with you. You've grown into a fine man."

"You like it up here so much, you want to die here."

It was a cruel, unthinking thing to say, and Eddard could see that Samuel was upset, and with good cause. He did not stop the younger man from leaving the tower where they spoke, descending the seventy eight steps, and walking off into the woods, leaving their conversation unfinished. The old man watched the younger become smaller and smaller until he disappeared from view entirely, obscured by the dark cover of the pine canopy.

Eddard looked out the windows by himself for the first time. He wondered how many hours had passed while Samuel's eyes were focused out these windows. He noted the undulations of the mountains, spread out like so many mounds of sugar upon a table. They looked close enough so that he could reach out and topple them. The river down below reflected the sun back at him with vengeance as the last of the day's light did its best to make itself known and remembered before its long sleep. Eddard stayed that way, waiting. It was long after dark before he heard Samuel's steps on the stairs again. When the young man walked into the room, Eddard offered no comment. He didn't need to, for Samuel himself spoke.

"I'll do it."

"Samuel you can…"

"But we need to talk logistics."

This was the voice of the fire lookout, the employee of the forestry service, and not the voice of his young friends.

"Who saw you in town?"

"Nobody. I made sure of it."

"Do you have a plan?"

"More than I laid out for you?"

"Yes. I want it on paper, written down properly. I need a guideline before you get too sick to write one. I trust that you're in your right mind right now, and that matters."

Eddard could see as well as anyone might that Samuel was shielding his feelings behind procedure, but the old man was in no position to halt the young man, who was granting his wish. In another time, Eddard would have urged Samuel to give voice to his internal thoughts, but though it pained him, he could not this time.

"Okay," was all he said. "I can do that."
For days, Eddard worked with an ash pencil in one of Samuel's notebooks, until he finally presented Samuel with a very brief, but ironclad document. Its instructions were simple: the first time Eddard asked for reprieve, it was to be granted. It stated clearly that he would not ask until he was certain, and that if he did, it was not to be questioned. It also requested, if it were possible, for him to be buried not under the shadow of an old tree, but under a very new one, no more than a few feet tall. Closing the notebook, Samuel nodded.

"Thank you."
"You shouldn't be the one thanking me."
"You chose me. There's an honor in that."
"I can't thank you."
"I wish you wouldn't."
"Very well."

9

The final month felt as if it were only days, perhaps hours, the early days of his visit never to be recovered. It seemed that the truth asserted itself once it was spoken out loud, and that Eddard had received a temporary reprieve by holding in the truth for so long on the mountain. After he was gone, Samuel wondered if Eddard would have lived forever had he simply refused to acknowledge his mortality. Milton had once told him that time spent on the tower didn't subtract from one's lifespan. Maybe he was right; if you believed in it.

In the end, it was rather quick. One day he was fine, and the next he was gasping. He told Samuel that it was time, and that he'd like to walk as far as he could, as to save Samuel carrying a body.

"Thoughtful, for a dead man."
"Not just yet," he rasped.

They barely made it down the winding, right-angled steps with Samuel guiding him down. Only the night before, sitting outside near a bonfire, the old man had seemed okay. They had played at chess, joking, coming as close as they had to those early days.

The old man had no poignant last words, or deathbed advice. When it came down to it, he didn't have the breath, even if he'd had the intention.

 Samuel could not hold the old man's anticlimactic death against him. Last words were overrated. Eddard Morley had said enough things to Samuel during his life, and he wasn't going to change that by a few final gurgles.

It took less morphine than he had imagined, and before ten am, the time fires were designated to be stopped, his heart had stopped beating. Considerate until the end, Samuel had the whole of the day to do his dirty work. As sunken as his body was, the old man was no more than ninety pounds, but dead weight is no joke. Samuel found an adequate tree, some three feet in height, not far from the tower, no more than a quarter mile below. Leaving

Eddard, he returned with his axe, again in trench-digging mode, and began his work. It was hard work, gravedigging, but it did have the effect of occupying his mind. It likely would have carried him through the task, the exhaustion doing its intended human work, had Samuel not been interrupted. He looked up to find that he was not alone.

Some fifty yards below was a black bear, ursus americanus. It stood on its hind legs and stared directly at Samuel, judging. The lookout remained still, waiting to see if the bear would come closer, or retreat. It did neither. It only remained, staring at Samuel as he stood waist deep in the earth, his friend's body nearby. For minute upon dragging minute, the standoff continued, the bear refusing to yield, Samuel remaining still. It was in this moment of inaction and silence that the young lookout was finally overwhelmed. From the moment he had woken up that morning, he had been busy in the act of killing and burying his friend. Now, the bear forced him to stop, to take stock, to reckon with what he had done. He hated the bear for it.

Tears rolled down Samuel's cheeks freely, and he did not try and wipe them. He stared straight ahead, through the bear and onwards down the mountain. His tears created streaks through his dusty, unwashed face, and a part of him wanted to lie down in the hole he had dug and give up. Samuel fell to his knees. He lay his head on the side of the grave and shook with emotion, the coolness of the upturned earth calming his feverish body. By the time he looked up again, the bear was gone.

In years to come, on rainy or otherwise particularly ponderous days, Samuel would wonder if the bear had been real, or simply a product of his grief. If he were prone to religious beliefs, perhaps he would have seen the spirit of his friend so soon reanimated before him. But Samuel was not that kind of man. Shuckstack was not a mystical place, but one of tremendous cruelty and beauty, of fire and smoke, and of death.

Part 3:

1976

1

In his thirty plus years of work at the Forestry Service, Samuel Meller was known as being a royal pain in the ass. The lifetime bureaucrats who just so happened to end up in the service did not know what they were getting into when the man who walked with a limp and carried a hickory cane came stumping into their office. He had hurt his leg many years before when he had been a lookout in the Gila. A rock slide had trapped his leg underneath thousands of pounds of mountainside. It was a miracle he was able to free himself at all, much less get back to his tower and radio for help. He was, despite the groans that his name elicited, a legend. There was never any doubt that when it came to field experience in forest fires, Samuel Meller was the guy to talk to. He was a frequent and unannounced guest to lookout fill-ins, popping in to make sure they were getting along, perhaps regaling them with a story that was longer than they really wanted. But none of the young, new lookouts were willing to tell off the middle- aged man who had served in their job for twenty five years.

It was not his time as a lookout and his reputation thereof that preceded Samuel when he walked into a forestry service office. It was the dozens of papers he had published over the years about the fire suppression policy of the United States Forest Service. Samuel proclaimed, loudly and often, that the "10 am" policy of the service was ill-conceived and not in the best interest of American wilderness. He argued that the constant suppression of fire did more harm than good, that for thousands, maybe millions of years before the forest service existed, the forests burned and revived themselves effectively. The burning was necessary in order to renew the soil and bring back the undergrowth necessary to a healthy forest. The suppression of fire was only putting off fires to a later date, building up unhealthy tinderboxes which would burn out of human control. He argued that the forest service was achieving exactly the opposite of its stated goal: best use. It was not the best use of the land, nor was it prudent.

Again and again, he used public forums to state that the forest service should systematically engage in intentional non-suppression of fires, letting them burn, granted that they did not endanger any humans of human property.

For many years, no one in the forest service particularly wanted to hear these counterintuitive ideas. Luckily, the science was starting to bear out what Samuel Meller had long known. Thirty five years after he left Shuckstack Mountain, a man came into Samuel Meller's New Mexico office. He was a scientist, and had spent years studying the soil of the American Southwest, and comparing it to nearly identical regions south of the border. He had reached the conclusion that Samuel had known he would: American land was not healthy. It needed to burn.

"How did you know way back when? When you started making noise about this, no one was even talking about it."

Samuel knew the answer to this question, because he had thought of it many times. He had been asked innumerable times where he got the idea, and his answer was always the same.

"A very good friend of mine told me as much, just before he passed away. Once he said it, it became clear as day. It was only my second year as a lookout. I was still real green around the gills. I'd spotted a couple dozen fires and seen action on exactly one of them."

"Action?"

"In those days, lookouts were expected to be first on the scene. I was just following directions. I was a young man, real sore about not being able to fight in the war. I saw following orders from the forestry service as my penance, my way of serving my country. It never occurred to me, until he told me so bluntly, that perhaps following my 10 am orders wasn't the best course of action."

"He must have been a smart man."

"He was. I won't deny it. One of the smartest I've ever known. But what's struck me so much about his explanation in the years since, is not his genius, but how intuitive it is. If fire was so bad, then why were there any forests at all? How had they not burnt away?"

"I think, Mr. Meller, we have difficulty. Humans I mean, thinking on the scale necessary to understand this sort of thing."

"Perhaps all scientists should be told they're dying."

"Pardon?"

"They say men on their deathbeds finally achieve perspective. If you're dying, you'd be more inclined to think in terms greater than your own lifespan."

The scientist smiled and picked up his coffee cup from Samuel's desk. The man from the forestry service had a cluttered workspace, maps strewn across his desk, older versions of those maps, lines not yet redrawn, hung from his walls. Stained coffee cups littered every service, and stacks of books were in every corner.

"They say lookouts are unusual, that they often say things like…well like what you've just said. Peculiar breed, lookouts. And yet here you are in an office with no windows."

Samuel closed his eyes and held his hands in the air like some kind of beat yogi, with his white beard and his thinning hair beneath his green service cap.

"It's all in here," he said."I've seen more skyline than most folks can fathom."

"Do you still...well-"

"I can't lookout anymore. Don't move fast enough. But do I go into the mountains? Of course. Wouldn't have any business working here if I didn't...although I can't say everyone in the service follows such guidelines. Now," he said. "I'm sure your time is more valuable than mine. Shall we get to the matter at hand?"

"Certainly. Let's."

The scientist reached underneath his chair and pulled a stack of papers from his briefcase.

"It's all in layman's language so that you can make everything very clear to the select committee yourself. As I explained on the phone-"

"And you're absolutely certain you can't testify yourself?"

"I'm sorry, Mr. Meller. I have commitments that must be maintained. Please understand, I hope you are successful in your efforts. I'm very much on your side."

"We'll see," Samuel said, less than confident after many years of fighting the same battle. "I can't thank you enough for allowing me to use your research."

"The pleasure is all mine, Mr. Meller."

In earlier days, Samuel might have taken the time to tell the man that his favorite kind of tree was named after a geologist: Benjamin Franklin Shumard, but Samuel had gotten at least slightly better at knowing when a fellow would not find something as interesting as he. The two men each rose from their chairs and shook hands. Samuel sat back in his chair, his feet up on his desk, thinking in silence for a long time. It had been years since he spent any time in a tower, but his habits still resembled those of a lookout. He spent most of his time alone, in silent contemplation. Soon, he would read over what the geologist had given him, though he hardly needed to. He had been following the man's research from the very beginning, hoping that he would be able to prove what Samuel knew to be true.

Samuel was testifying in front of a select committee of congress, created after the conclusion of the Vietnam War. Much like after the second world war, and Korea, the military had a massive surplus of equipment, and it was up to each department to present proposals as to why theirs should receive something from the surplus. It was Samuel's hope that the forestry service could gain more helicopters. There were already helicopters in the service. They were used to drop fire fighters into blazes to do battle. But Samuel had other ideas. With more choppers in the air, fire surveillance, not suppression, would be an easier, and perhaps more palatable task. He planned to present the committee with scientific evidence that showed the forests were in need of "controlled" burns. He would present the esteemed statesmen with evidence that suggested by allowing some fires to burn, catastrophic fires like the McKnight Fire of 1951 could be avoided. Samuel knew it was an uphill battle. Even with the evidence on his side, it was no easy task to convince folks that they ought to let fires burn. It goes against human nature, to relinquish control, but he was determined.

2

Samuel had found what his father, Tom Meller had always wanted him to have: drive. Unfortunately, the old man had not lived to see his son find his true calling and passion, and had died still bitter at his son. It was one of Samuel's biggest regrets in life, and his mother constantly told him to forgive himself, but it was difficult.

"He would be proud," She told him last time he had made it to Ohio. "Just know that."

Samuel had not been at his father's funeral, as it had taken place during his wandering. After leaving Shuckstack Mountain in early 1943, unable to remain there any longer, Samuel had taken a number of lookout assignments all over the United States, though nothing could take the place in his heart of the mountains of the American Southeast. They had imprinted themselves on his soul. Samuel had apprised no one of his whereabouts during those early post-war years. His father had died of a heart attack in 1946, while Samuel was in Gila, New Mexico.

Samuel wasn't aware of his father's death until nearly two years later when he sent a letter to his mother from the hospital. He had been in an accident, injured his leg, but he was fine he told her. The doctors told him it would affect him more and more with age, and would likely be debilitating eventually. But for the time being, once he was recovered, he intended to be back on the peak. In her return letter, his mother had begged him to come home for a time, to recover back on the farm with her.

He had relented, and boarded a train for Ohio, headed back to his home state for the first time in nearly a decade. He watched the vegetation out the window once more, saw it thinning out in real time, revealing the rolling plains of middle america where his beloved trees had been before. Over the years, his appreciation for growing up on a property with trees had grown. He was at least looking forward to seeing the south wood once more, even if many of his memories there would be painful to him now.

When the man came round to punch his ticket, Samuel felt a pang of unexpected grief at the young face that greeted him, smiling goofily and showing crooked teeth.

"Does an old man work on this train line?"

"What?"

The youth had an expressionless, bovine face that did not betray any deep thinking.

"An old man. I rode this line years ago, and there was an old man who punched tickets."

"Just me who punches the tickets as far as I know. But there are probably more. I don't really know. Just punch my clock and then punch tickets."

"Thanks," Samuel said quietly, the pain in his leg suddenly feeling much worse than it had only moments before.

Grief suited his mother. This was the first thought Samuel had upon seeing her, and guilt immediately followed. Her mourning clothes were well-cut, fashionable, and slimming. It was almost as if she had been forced to wait until her husband died to reach her full potential, as Tom

Meller had never been a man to advocate spending money on something like clothes. Samuel mentally upbraided himself for such a thought. He had committed himself to honoring the memory of his father as best he could after the guilt of not being around for his death. But the thought came unbidden. It was undeniable. His mother looked refreshed in a way he could hardly remember. On her head, she wore a well-stitched, custom hat. She embraced her son as soon as he dropped his bag on the front porch, before he even had an opportunity to get in the door.

"Rude of me," she muttered, wringing her hands and standing awkwardly in the living room, unsure of how to proceed. "Forgive me. You're such a man now. You were only a boy when you left us."

"I was eighteen."

"Just a boy. Look at you now, your beard. Your...darling is your leg okay?"

Samuel's limp, even aided by his smart cane, was more pronounced in small spaces, and his mother's face bore genuine concern for her son's well being.

"It's so dangerous up there, you know."

"You think I'd have been safer in France somewhere?"

Samuel immediately regretted his ill-tempered comment. He had been travelling all day, his leg ached, but it was no excuse to say something like that. So many lives had been lost, and his little hometown had not been spared the bloodshed. A number of the town's young men had lost their lives in faraway places, and many others had come back forever changed, physically or otherwise.

"Forgive me."

"Forgive us both," his mother said. "We've been apart for so long, we don't know how to be in the same room anymore. Don't think of it."

"To tell you the truth, I'm not much good a being in the same room as anyone," Samuel said some minutes later, seated at the kitchen table while his mother put on the kettle. "I've spent the better part of the last decade by myself. I'm sure I'll be terrible company."

"You're injured. I'm your mother. You'll be welcome company is what you'll be."

3

Neither of them was willing to broach the subject of Tom Meller, his passing, or the fact that his son had been off his family's radar during that cataclysmic event. When they spoke of the past, they delicately tiptoed around events in which his father had taken part, which was most events as he had been the farm's patriarch.

"Mostly just empty fields now," she said. "I've had a few folks come by and ask to rent out plots from me, but I don't know. I'm comfortable enough, and I'm no young woman myself. I can't see the need. I like the look of the place as it returns to the wild."

Her eyes were cast out the kitchen window on the fields that did in fact look as if they were returning to the wild. They had not been cleared for planting and they had a certain derelict charm. It was in this moment that Samuel realized for the first time all that he had in common with his mother. It was from her blood that he found his affinity for the outdoors. It may not have manifested itself quite as violently in her, as the duties of a woman when she was of marrying age and the growing pragmatism of a farmer's wife had colluded to drive it partially from her mind, but there in that moment Samuel could see in her the same reverence for wildness that he held dear to his own heart.

"I like the look of it too," Samuel said. "It's all yours now. Don't let any of the men in town tell you what to do."

"Oh you don't have to worry about that. I like it the way it is, and I'll keep it just so. All this land was like the south of the property not so long ago. That was always your place. You spent your brooding youth in those woods."

"Mother, I was not a brooding youth."
At this, his mother actually laughed heartily enough that she was forced to set down her tea on the table as not to spill all over herself.

"I don't know how you remember those years, but you were certainly a brooding, young man. Not that there's anything wrong with that. It's all perfectly natural. You would sulk with your books, rubbing your hands along trees. All very dramatic."

"I still run my hands along trees. I never knew you saw me."

"Well it's hardly the forest at the end of the world. I can see most of the woods from my bedroom window. Saw you bring your young crushes out there too. Oh yes, young boys always think they're so clever."

"Just Amelia. I never brought anyone else."

Samuel knew that his mother had been deliberately obtuse by using the phrase she had chosen, but he still felt the need to correct her, though the genuine shock of her words made it more difficult. Had she always been able to see all that? It was funny how much he imagined he had learned about himself, and yet he still held onto such clear memories that were evidently not wholly the truth.

"I'll have to go out there again. Somehow, your description of it does not match up with what I remember."

"Of course it doesn't. As I said, you were just a boy. Take a walk in the wood, you'll see what I mean. One more thing...be careful. She still gathers feathers there you know."

"Amelia?"

"She has her own store now. I let her get feathers. She made the hat I'm wearing in fact. She's done quite well for herself."

"I'm glad to hear it."

"Her husband lost his arm, and quite a bit of his mind. Shouts sometimes at the least noise."

"I don't need to know these things. Town gossip doesn't interest me."

"Not gossip, son. I just want you to know what you ran away from. People here suffered greatly, and some well…"

"Well what?"

"There are those who say some unkind things. About your leaving, I mean."

"You're saying the town thinks I'm some kind of coward?"

"I tell about your vision, but you know how things are. People died. There's a certain bitterness. We are fragile creatures, in the end."

"Amelia thinks I'm a coward?"

"I said no such thing. I wouldn't know the first thing about what she thinks of you, and I don't think you ought to either. I only wanted you to be prepared for a few things. You ought to just focus on healing."

"Of course."

And Samuel did focus on healing. He and his mother gradually fell into a rhythm, able to accept each other into their respective daily routines for the first time in many years. They would have breakfast together, stopping afterwards to have pressed coffee on the porch. The senior Meller would head to town, while the younger would grab his cane so that he could exercise his leg as the doctor told him he must. It was never without fear that Samuel re-entered the the south wood, wonderland of his childhood. Each time, he worried that he would find a ghost, finding feathers as he had taught her. The wood itself had shrunk, as his mother had known, an area of ground that would have been negligent to him atop the tower, but had made up the basis for his love of the outdoors. From the creek, which had always seemed mysteriously deep into the forest, an alcove away from the farm, the back porch could be viewed through the branches in the middle of the afternoon when there was enough light. Samuel came to terms with his memories as all are forced to do at some point. He came out on the other side with his appreciation for the wood undiminished. Altered yes, but his appreciation was greater if changed at all. Such a small place to his lookout's practiced eye, and yet it contained so much.

He still rubbed his hands along the same trees he had done as a child and as a man in the smokies, a young man with a cane revisiting the past. Samuel could not deny the strangeness of his walks. He was amazed to find that not so much time had passed after all. To the wood, ten years was but a moment. He found his favorite trees nearly imperceptibly changed, their time scale on this earth on a

much longer arc than Samuel's. The creek ran in the same path as ever before, the bushes remained unchecked.
On one of these days spent in the wood, Samuel came back to find his mother sitting on the steps of the back porch, waiting for him to return. She looked tired.

"Your father spent a lot of time out there after you left."

"He did?"

"Oh yes. He was a very proud man. Like his son," she added.

"May be the only thing we have in common."

"Every son thinks that at one point or another, but you're more like your father than you know. He loved this land. So much that I felt jealous at times. Tom had a reverence for this place that never made sense to me."
But it made sense to Samuel. Reverence for land was something he understood very well. He spit in his father's face by turning up his nose at the land that was theirs and finding his greatest appreciation for the natural world elsewhere. It was a great betrayal of Tom Meller.

"I'm sorry I didn't come back, mom."

"Well you're here now. That's what matters."

He did not bring books to the wood as he had before, as he found himself unable to concentrate for long. It was a condition that had first presented itself after his accident. His mind was always in need of distraction, and did not sit still for long as it had always done. It was the dull ache of his leg that always drew him back to the present, the pages of a book unable to disappear such reality. Constant motion and constant activity were Samuel's only respite from the constancy of pain. He thought to himself rather begrudgingly that he was in no shape to be a lookout at present. He would be a poor lookout, unable to sit still for long. Only on his darkest days, his mother in town or playing at cards, rain more likely than not pattering against the tin roof of the farmhouse, did Samuel wonder if he would ever again return to the mountains as a lone sentinel. He had been kept on after the war, but their numbers were not so shallow now that men had returned en masse to the country. Perhaps his services would no longer be needed by the forestry service. It was in these moments that he sometimes thought of Amelia as she had been ten years past, first as a salve, but inevitably as a further stab of pain to his already tormented mind.

4

As his time back home wore on, the absence of Amelia became more pronounced in Samuel's mind. It had been his biggest concern in spending any time in the entirety of the state of Ohio, and after being home a month in his small hometown, he had not come any closer to her than seeing the parade of ever-fancier hats that his mother seemed to have acquired in the time since he had seen her. Samuel noticed that he only thought of Amelia when he was already in a state of emotion conducive to self destruction. He rarely thought of her when he was walking in the woods, or in those moments when he was able to read some few pages in peace before his mind interrupted, but only as a kick to his rear when already upset. Samuel was beginning to understand something of the effects of time. In truth, if he was to look himself in the mirror and speak honestly, he could not say that he felt anything for Amelia anymore. Samuel was sad for certain, but not about her. He hadn't been for a long time. He was upset that his chosen life was in jeopardy, and the human mind simply has a way of bringing up all past hurts when they are most inconvenient, and into this category Amelia fell. It was something of a revelation. For years, Samuel had held onto a belief that he had lost his great love, and that though it had been his own fault, this he accepted readily, the truth of the loss was unshakeable. Now he was forced to face the idea that time, solitude, and communion with his mountains had healed his wound, and that maybe she had not been his only chance at love. She could fall into the very same category as the south wood, looming so large in Samuel's memory alone, the reality being quite different. His mother came home one evening from her canasta game and found Samuel listening to the Cardinals on the radio.

"When I was in the tower out west, I could pick up Cardinals games on the radio. I could never find any teams closer by, the more logical answer, but the St. Louis AM was always as clear as a bell. I probably knew more about the Cardinals than any resident of St. Louis that year. I listened to nearly a hundred games."
There was a smile on Samuel's face that his mother couldn't quite place.

"How's your leg?" she asked.

"Doing better. Or at least I'm getting better at ignoring it."

"Amounts to about the same thing doesn't it?"

"I suppose it does."

His mother sat down next to him on the couch and listened to the baseball game. During the seventh inning stretch they got bread and butter from the kitchen and returned to their place on the couch. In the top of the ninth, they started a fire in the grate. When the game was still tied at three at the top of the eleventh, they traded yawns back and forth. Finally, in the bottom of the thirteenth, Schoendienst hit one out and Samuel and his mother cheered as loudly as the people in the stadium all those miles away. When the radio was turned off, and all was silent in the Meller house, his mother was the first to speak.

"You know that's the first game I ever listened to like that?"

"What do you mean? Dad listened to games all the time. I remember."

"I found things to do. I cleaned dishes, folded laundry. Boring things I could have done any old time. I never sat down and listened with him."

"Mom."

"Not once."

She was crying now, tears streaming down her face freely. It was the first naked display of emotion Samuel had seen her give about his father since he had returned. He drew her close to him and let her cry into his shoulder, able to offer that at least, though knowing not what to say. Countless times in his childhood, she had comforted him, but when the tables were turned, he was at a loss. Still, when she was finished she thanked him and wiped her face with dignity on his sleeve.

"When's the next game?" she said. "I think I'd like to listen with you."

"Tomorrow night, mom."

"Good," she said. "I'm going to go to bed now, dear. Sleep well."

5

Before his hearing before the select congressional committee, Samuel was thinking about his time back home after his accident. It had been the first important bookend in his life. A man needs bookends, conclusions to periods in his life on which he can later look back and see where things changed. His convalescence at home was certainly one of these moments for Samuel. He had reconciled with his mother and with his past, and it had allowed him to move forward with life. He had let go of Amelia, stopped pretending as if she had been the end of his romantic life, and he eventually found love again.

Her name was Patricia and she was his weekend relief lookout when he returned to the Gila after his accident. While Samuel remembered crisply the amazement in which he had held Amelia's beauty, his first impressions of Patricia were quieter, and had remained so. She was a small woman, her nose so aquiline as to nearly disappear at its peak. Her eyes were brown and close together, her hair forever chopped short. She reminded Samuel of a northern conifer, not a delicate flower. This was much superior. He held for her a tremendous respect and admiration, an awe of her power and beauty, but no fear of crushing her petals underfoot by accident.

By that time, the service was offering two days off every ten and Samuel felt compelled to take them most times. The first time Patricia arrived to relieve him for the weekend, he nearly fell from the tower.

"Ho there!" she shouted, coming through the lookout door.

Samuel was so startled that he tripped over his own stool and tumbled forward, cracking the window. He spluttered wordlessly as his new relief lookout pulled him back by the collar of his shirt.

"Were you raised in a barn?" Samuel said.

"I assumed you'd have seen me approaching."

"I've been keeping tabs on the Relief Fire. Look."

He walked gingerly back towards the window and showed her the steady, rising smoke coming from a valley many miles away in the Mogollons.

"Named for moi?"

"Well, had you knocked me out the window, I think a renaming would be in order, but since all's well."

"I'll name my first after you as a thank you." Samuel laughed.

"That won't be necessary. There have been enough fires around here with my mark on them. Don't think we need anymore. I think I'd settle for your name. That way, next time I can name one more properly in your honor."

"Patricia."

"Samuel."

She was a wonderful woman, loved the mountains like he did, and they fit together so well it was as if they had always been meant to spend days together. Sometimes they'd go hours without speaking, but it suited them both equally, and they'd come out of silence to make love in high altitude. His love with Patricia had none of the high drama of novels or of young love, but that did not make it less valuable. They were comfortable together, and that rated higher in Samuel's book than drama.

"Do you ever worry that we don't do enough?" she asked him once very early in their relationship. She was still his relief, though he was spending many of his free weekends with her on the mountain.

"We hiked fifteen miles today, Pat. I think that's a fair stretch. Nothing to scoff at."

"No, I mean normal stuff. We don't go to the movies, or to city council meetings, or weekly grocery trips. What if we're missing out on something important?"

"Is that what you think? Do you think those things are important? Is that why you're bringing it up?"

"No, I don't. I really don't."

"I can't see why anyone would choose those over this."

"Neither can I, Samuel."

There were difficult times, of course. The manner of their first meeting should have acted as a premonition for them that not everything would be basalt-smooth. There were plenty of times when the tower in the Gila was too small for the both of them, when it became the sight of some of their fiercest arguments, the blaze of anger not contained by the small space, but exacerbated.

"Drop it," Samuel said, his eye catching on the crack in the window behind Patricia, the physical marker of their first meeting.

"No. Someone has to make you act like an adult."

"I've been on my own-"

"Since you left home in a fit of adolescent stupidity. I know the story, Samuel and in a lot of ways you've matured since then. Your time alone has served you well in some areas, but in others...not so much."

"I'm doing fine."

"You need to write home."

"I haven't had time."

"That's bullshit and you know it. Look what happened with your father. You brooded alone and what did you get to show for it? Write to your mother."

Patricia did not quite know the festering wound she had poked. Samuel's guilt at his father's passing and his own absence was immense. He did not reply to Patricia, but turned on his heel and left the tower, not to return for hours.

It was dark and Patricia was drinking tea and leafing through a book of Tennyson when Samuel returned. He did not apologize or explain his absence.

"Do we have any of that good paper?"
"I keep some in the nightstand drawer."
Samuel grunted.

Their wedding was a small affair, neither of them having much in the way of family, and each of them with only a few close friends. Samuel's mother wore a heron-plume hat that obscured Samuel's view of his wedding guests while he and his mother danced together. Blynne Meller cried openly but quietly for her son.

"She's wonderful, Samuel. I love you both."
"Thank you, mother. You look beautiful."
His mother sniffed loudly.
"You were never much of a liar. I saw how you looked at my hat."

"It's not exactly couth anymore to-"

"Oh let me be, Samuel. I'm an old lady now. I'll do as I like."

Samuel smiled broadly and wondered if this woman had always been present, and he had simply missed her. Was he too dull in his youth to notice what a firecracker his mother was, or had his father's influence made her a different person? His memory was no help.

After the ceremony, the bride and groom were in a cramped hotel suite in Cleveland that suited neither of them, but had been generously booked by Samuel's mother. They sat naked in the bathtub across from each other, their legs intertwined in a column of foam.

"What now then?" Patricia asked, taking a sip of champagne from a stemmed glass.

"I'd say leaving Cleveland as fast as possible ought to be a priority."

"Naturally, but after that."

"We're both on assignment in two weeks, so I'd say a lot of looking out windows for both of us."

"After that, even."

"I've never been to Europe."

"Do you regret it? That you never saw the wonders of the old world as a child?"

"A little."

"We'll wait a few years then, bring the baby when they're old enough to remember."

"You're a wise woman. I knew there was a reason I married you."

"I'd always thought it was because I nearly knocked you out of your tower."

"Well, there's rarely only one reason for a thing."

There was no trip to Europe, as there were no babies.

"I can't do it," Samuel said. "I just can't."

"You *can't* have sex with me? What's that supposed to mean?"

"I don't mean that. I mean not like this, planning it out like stage managers."

"That's how it's done, Samuel. I'm sorry that I can't always ovulate when you feel struck by the beauty of the moment."

"Fine."

It was not fine, and things only worsened. As an older man, Samuel regretted how much their futile attempts to bring life into the world strained their relationship. The stress was overwhelming. For three years the young couple tried to have children and for three years they lived tense, high-strung lives. When it was all over, when they had called it quits, they went on a vacation, and took a long hiking trip together in the Yosemite. Neither of them had been to Muir's favorite cathedral before, and it seemed the right time.

They hiked all day, their packs rubbing uncomfortably against their shoulders, until they reached a peak with a view of Cathedral Peak. The great stone peak stood out against a nighttime sky beginning to erupt, with a blood moon at center. A few trees trimmed the lower edges of the peak, but all the hustle and bustle of nature was largely left in the shadow of the beast. The married couple sat against their packs, their hands silently intertwined against the cool rock surface on which they sat. For a long time they sat, allowing the nighttime noises of Yosemite to overtake them. A stream not far away bubbled quietly, crickets chirped, and a lone owl hooted, its voice carried across the vastness of the valley. Slowly, Patricia edged towards her husband and leaned her weight against him. Her head found his shoulder, and she unraveled. Samuel held tightly as her thin body shook against him violently, racked by sobs.

They spoke little the first night in Yosemite, but Patricia's voice eventually returned. A day later, they were in the valley over which they had watched the night before. Patricia, who was walking ahead of Samuel put her arm out to stop him.
    "There's a bear."
She did not point, but Samuel saw it. *Ursus Americanus.*
    "What did you say?"
Samuel had not realized he had spoken aloud.

"I've run into one before."
The bear was fishing, and the couple looked on, amazed as the bear deftly swatted a fish out of the water and onto a sandbank. It quickly devoured the creature before starting the exercise over again.

"I'm a lookout too, Samuel. We've all seen bears."

"I saw one when my best friend died. I buried him, and the bear was there, just watching me."

"You've never told me that."

"For a long time I wasn't sure if it even happened, if I hadn't dreamed it."

On their trip to Yosemite, Samuel began telling Eddard's story. he had always left him out of the narrative before. Samuel had never shied away from telling Patricia of Amelia and what she had meant to him, but Eddard he kept for himself.

"Homeless?"

"He knew he was only a burden to his wife, so he lit out in search of work to send her money."

"And she married someone else while he was gone?"

"That's about the shape of it."

"He must have been bitter."

"Eddard wasn't one to be bitter."

"Sad then."

"Very much so."

Patricia clung to Eddard's story with more fervor than Samuel could have imagined. Far from being jealous of the amount of space he occupied in her husband's thoughts, she wanted the whole story, and Samuel would give it to her over their years together. They were able to share Eddard's story, a couple in need of something precious and close-kept.

"I'm really sorry," Patricia said.

"It's okay. It was a long time ago."

"It's horrible to see death so up close that young."

"I grew up on a farm. I knew about death."

"But not like that."

"No, not like that."

"You were angry at him."

"Very. You have to understand, I thought he was some kind of beat Jesus. I was a kid."

"You never entirely grew out of it did you? Even when you knew he lost a family, a job, was alone, there was something larger than life about him. It comes through in all the things you say about him, what you choose to say, how well you remember your conversations."

"Until the end. You didn't see him. He was skin and bones. I felt guilty burying him. It was stronger than my grief, this idea that I'd never really known him."

"Can't blame yourself entirely. He tried to protect you."

"He did. For a long time."

They had been married for ten years before the lump appeared in Patricia's breast. She was only thirty seven years old. She took the news with her typical stoicism, even when they took one breast, then the other, she remained solid, much more so than Samuel.

"You're only thirty seven," he'd say repeatedly.

"I know how old I am, Samuel."

"It just doesn't make sense."

"Sure it makes sense. It's not *fair,* but you can't say it doesn't make sense. It makes perfect sense."

It wasn't until the end that she became scared. By then she was a shell, no more than eighty pounds, a child in an adult bed. She breathed through tubes and her room's window looked out on a parking lot.

"I'm scared," she said point blank.

"It's gonna be okay."

"You don't have to say that, Samuel. I know it's not true. That's why I'm so scared. I'm scared because I know now it's not going to be okay."

He had not reached the bookend on that period in his life just yet. After her passing, he again spent some time with his mother, though the death of a wife is not as easily solved as the bad breaking of a leg. After that, he poured himself into his work, becoming the hell-raising forestry service figure that he was known as now. He spent most of his time in an office without windows, writing about forests and mountains he knew so well as to write elegantly and passionately at his typewriter without so much has strolling outside to see the sun. They were in him and part of him.

The former lookout discovered love twice in the wild, and would never be able to repay his debt to it, though he tried through one fiery essay after another. The first time it was with an old man, someone with whom he shared nothing in common, and yet had an outsized effect on his life. Patricia, of course the other love, had always understood the reverence in which her husband spoke of the old man who had needed him to die. She was the only person to whom he had ever told the whole story. She understood him in that way, and so of course she had to leave him too.

There had been no drama with a bear when she had passed, only the sprinkling of ashes in a few places Samuel thought were beautiful, per her request. She had died as she had lived, quietly, and without much trouble, a steward in lieu of a burden.

6

The former lookout's cane echoed on the hardwood as he walked to his committee hearing. It was appropriate, he thought, that the legacy of his love for those people, and for the woods that had brought them to him at last was to be fire. Samuel knew now that fire was not a devious force of evil in the world, as he had first thought all those years ago, stumping down the mountain with his axe to do proxy battle with his own germans. No, it was a cleansing force, clearing the way for newer, richer soil, and even greater forests of years long after all the current forestry service employees were dead.

"Well," the bald-pated congressman said. "Mr. Meller you make a compelling argument, and I see no reason to disbelieve you, but I must be frank. The public will not take this in stride."

"Sir?"

"You're asking us to announce that instead of fighting fires, we're going to let them burn?"

"No sir, I'd not phrase it just like that."

There were some laughs in the chamber, but Samuel's face remained resolute.

"It's management sir. No people will be endangered unnecessarily. Fires nearest to towns and roads will be fought just as before. My point is that it will be beneficial to our grandchildren if we do not fight...all the fires with such vigor. Army helicopters can help ensure the efficacy of my plan. If it suits the committee, I'd not object to the simple declaration that the US Army is kindly donating helicopters to the forestry service in order to continue their good work."

"You ought to have been a politician," the congressman said.

"My constituents have historically been very large, furry, and opposed to voting, sadly."

Again, laughter in the chambers. It was not the first time Samuel had lobbied in public, though this was the largest scale. He had gotten much better at speaking in public by necessity. Whenever he saw his mother again, she always brought up his improved conversational skills, and they compared favorably to when he had stayed with her after his accident.

"The committee appreciates your presentation. We have several more parties to hear from before our deliberation."

"Thank you," Samuel said.

He didn't need to wait to know what their decision was going to be. They had laughed at his jokes, and had appreciated him as some odd creature who had spent much of his life alone, cultivating odd ideas, but they would not approve his request. It was not a winning move for them, no matter what spin Samuel suggested. The fight would continue, and he would keep fighting for what he knew to be the best course of action, whatever the government's official edict on the matter happened to be. In fact, counter to orders, Samuel had been convening with some of the most experienced lookouts and feeling them out on taking matters into their own hands. A few had been open to reporting fires a bit late if they were in open wood and not in danger of causing damage. It was a start, but real change would require the cooperation of the service at large.

After his testimony, Samuel was tired, his leg was aching, and he was not pleased to see a man waiting for him at his office door. It was a young man, acne scars on his cheeks, and he looked nervous.

"Urgent telegram, sir."

"A mountain fall down?"

"Sir."

"Otherwise there's a cot in here that's waiting for me."

The young man shoved the piece of paper into Samuel's hands and walked away hastily, his hands in his pockets. He waited until he sat at his desk, his reading spectacles perched on the bridge of his nose, to unfold the piece of paper. It was as he had expected since the young man had fairly well run away from him. He folded his glasses and set them down on his desk before sighing deeply. He was going home to Ohio once more.

•••

If there was any lingering animus towards Samuel in his hometown for decisions he had made more than thirty years before, he could not detect when he returned to town.

"She was a wonderful lady," they said. "Always lit up the room."

"We all loved her," and other vulgarities that are spoken whenever anyone passes, no matter if they were the town drunk or the town banker. In regards to his mother, Samuel was inclined to believe most of the sentiments however. As an adult, he had come to not simply respect his mother as a child is inclined to do, but to see her as the remarkable person she was. Even though it would have resulted in the lack of his existence, Samuel could not help but feel his mother would have done extraordinary things had she never married Tom Meller. She never expressed any regrets, and loved Tom always, and it was not Samuel's place, here or ever to judge his mother's decisions in that regard. Her later years had been filled with a social life she had never known as a young or married woman. She had become a town fixture: serving on boards, donating money to schools, founding women's groups, and many more things. Despite the changes in fashion which put her hats firmly in the realm of out of style, and which caused Amelia Fribley to make her money mostly on alterations, the old woman could always be seen in the most fabulous hats. She had cloches, and flop-ears, and feminine fedoras she wore at jaunty angles. She was likely the only person who still asked Amelia to make hats like that, as the fashion of the time was drab colors which she found terribly depressing.

7

Samuel spent the better part of forty eight hours getting the arrangements together, running around a town he hadn't spent much time in in many years, talking to folks who all remembered him as a boy, trying to get out before the conversation trapped him and he was late to get the next thing: the flowers, the preacher, whatever it might have been. His mother had religiously attended the baptist church they had gone to when Samuel was a child, and so the service was to be held there. There weren't so many baptists in town, so the church was much too big for the small services it inevitably held. For his mother's funeral, Samuel instructed the church to leave the doors open. They could fill all the pews if that was necessary.

"If it was up to me, I'd invite only a few folks," he told the preacher. "But I know my mother would want it this way. She was always more outgoing than her son."

"Right you are, Samuel. You're a good son."

"Learned to be, anyway. Thank you, Pastor, for everything."

The morning of the service was the first time that Samuel cried. They were quiet tears, and he wiped them quickly as they came. When they had passed, he put on his one suit, the same suit he had been wearing in front of the congressional committee, and walked out his front door. He could drive to the church, but he felt like walking. It was a cool morning, and wet. Fog hung in the air, and Samuel couldn't see much more than six feet in front of his face. It felt like he was back on Shuckstack, trying to see through the clouds to the blue ridge. He thought his mother would appreciate a morning like this. As they had gotten closer after Tom Meller's passing, his mother had always shown a keen interest in hearing about her son's time spent in small towers by himself, way away from the world. She had asked detailed questions, and even showed a particular interest in the book of trees he had kept while there. After a few years, he had no longer needed to keep the book, being able to identify trees quite well on his own.

"A paper birch?" she asked one day, squinting through her glasses. "Is that what this says?"

"I remember that, actually. It was just off the trail that went back down to the village. I was amazed as well. They're native to Canada."

"How do you suppose it got there?"

"I don't know, mom. I've not thought about it in years."

"I'll ask Fred at the library. It's just the sort of thing he'd love to try and figure out for me."

Samuel smiled at the memory. It was just like his mother. A curious woman until she died, and few things are more complementary to a person as far as Samuel was concerned. The turnout for the funeral was even larger than expected. As a man accustomed to being alone, even when he is not emotional, it was more than a little overwhelming to Samuel. He rubbed his sweaty palms together and told himself it was for her. Every pew was full, and there was a crowd of people standing behind the last row and all the way to the door. The pastor had to ask for silence before beginning, the quiet murmurings of so many people caused enough of a dull roar.

The service itself was unremarkable, and Samuel had never much cared for funerals anyway. They always struck him as vulgar somehow, despite their pretensions to the opposite. He spoke but little, telling of how his mother and him liked to listen to the Cardinals together on the radio. He said it just like that, as a matter of fact. It was not an anecdote told to share an important truth about his mother, or about their relationship. It was a fact. They had liked to listen to baseball together,and now they couldn't. That was how death was. It did not impart wisdom. Samuel offered nothing more than a thank you to those who had come out. He had always known she was loved, and though he spent little time in Ohio anymore, he felt loved. The last bit wasn't true, but it was his one surrender to the ceremonies of death.

She was buried next to Tom shortly after the service. A drizzly rain fell and considerably less people trekked through the rain into the old cemetery to watch the casket lowered into the ground by a piece of farming equipment that had been owned by the deceased, and loaned out to the town on a permanent basis. Afterwards, Samuel did his duty, sticking around to shake hands and accept hugs he didn't want, to listen to people he didn't know talk about his mother and the relationship they had shared. A few were even rude enough to ask what he was going to do with the land, seeing as he didn't live here anymore. Was he going to sell?

It wasn't until the line of well-wishers came near an end that he recognized the woman about his own age who came to offer her condolences. She had aged well, much better than Samuel himself, and wore a black sheath mourning dress. She looked to Samuel, though it seemed implausible at best, more beautiful than when they had been teenagers.

"I'm very sorry, Samuel. She was a wonderful woman. She kept the shop afloat more than once I'm ashamed to say."

"I think she loved you. She never told me so, as to protect my feelings, but I think she loved you. She never had a daughter."

"And I a mother. I'd be proud to think of her in that way."

"She'd be glad to hear it."

There was an awkward silence between the two of them. There was such a history between them that had been dulled by years, but did not cease to exist. It was not the proper moment for it to be discussed either, but it was inevitably on their minds, no matter what shame that might have incurred upon them.

"A few of her closest friends are coming over for coffee," Samuel said by way of invitation. "This afternoon around three."

8

Samuel had little opportunity to have serious conversation with anyone at the small gathering at his parents' home. He spent his time brewing coffee, serving it, brewing some more, and listening to yet another story with infinite patience. The small group was mostly older ladies, this not being the first time one of their number had passed. Though middle-aged, Amelia and Samuel were almost certainly the youngest people there. They made eye contact a number of times, and Samuel shrugged when she tried to speak to him but he was pulled away. As the number dwindled, off to tend to their husbands or their hanging plants, Amelia lingered. Eventually, though it took hours of patience, the two were alone for the first time in more than thirty years.

"You're a good host," she offered.

At this, Samuel laughed and sat down in what had long ago been his father's chair.. Amelia sat across from him on the couch.

"I'm not."

"Then you should have gone into acting."

"My true calling, certainly. Did you hear Estelle asking me about the property?"

She looked down at her coffee cup, held with both hands.

"I'm not surprised. Everyone's been talking about it. Have been for years really."

"She never told me what she wanted me to do."

"She was a realistic woman."

"I don't think I'm going to sell it."

"You mean you're going to stay?"

"No, I don't mean that. I think I might donate it to the state nature conservancy. Just let the land return to its natural state."

"Folks would hate you."

"You forget. I don't live here."

"That's true. You never wanted to. You got your wish I suppose."

"My wish? No, I don't think so. I got something else entirely. I don't even know what I wanted then, really. I've thought about it a lot over the years, but it's a bit useless really. Why try to figure out what an eighteen year old wanted? I'm sure I didn't know. I can't deny that the way I left was stupid, but it's lead to a lot of good for me. I don't think leaving was the problem. I was meant to do that. On that I was correct. The manner could have been improved."

"Do you remember what you told me about lying on your back in the creek?"

"I don't."

"You said that you felt trapped, and that powerlessness was your greatest fear. Perhaps that will help you understand yourself from back then a little better."

"Afraid of powerlessness, from the boy who wanted to go to war. That's rather rich isn't it?"

"None of us knew what war was going to be like. Can hardly blame yourself."

"I'm...I'm sorry. I shouldn't have brought that-"

"You didn't mean anything by it. He was never the same after he came back. I don't think I'd have made it if it weren't for your mother. She got me through that ordeal."

Silence engulfed the room, neither of them willing to speak again, lest they say something wrong or insensitive. It was Amelia who broke the silence once more.

"You know I've read your articles."

"You have a lot of interest in forestry service policy?"

"Your mother showed some of them to me. She was very proud you know. She was always telling everyone about how her son was going to prove fire was good."

"Well, that's certainly an image."

"Something struck me about it, and I've wanted to tell you. You've conquered your greatest fear. Fire makes man powerless, and you seek to embrace it."

"I guess that's true. What about you?"

"What do you mean?"

"Have you conquered your fears?"

"No, I don't think so. Not yet."

...

"I'm sorry that I didn't respond to your letters."

"Don't be."

"We were so young."

"You always understood that better than I did. She always said you were smarter than me. She was always right too."

"I wanted to hurt you, then. And I apologize."

"I apologize."

"I suppose that's settled then. How would some more coffee suit you?"

...

They parted this time without tears, but with exchanged addresses, and the promise to write.

Five years later.

Although Samuel was vindicated, his fire policy finally going into effect this summer, he had not been up in a tower for several years. He simply couldn't manage the job for more than a few days at a time. So when, several weeks earlier, there was a knock at his office door, the news that reached him had been surprising. It was Sherman, one of the newer guys who had grown up being taught enough in science and history class to know that Samuel had always been right about forestry.

"Boss man, you got a second?"

"More than you can count. They've really kicked it into gear around here. I think they don't want to piss me off."

"Well after calling you crazy for thirty years…"

"Success does have its perks, though mine are mostly sloth. Come in, have a seat and let me know what I can do for you?"

"Thanks," Sherman said, sitting down in front of the cluttered desk. "And it's actually about something you might be able to do for me."

"Oh really?"

"Yeah, I got a call this morning from my guy down in Asheville. Seems that one of their weekend guys took off without notice. They're trying to replace him."

"But bureaucracy being what it is…"

"Exactly. And the lookout wants to see his wife."

"Understandably."

"Is it true that you started as a lookout at Shuckstack in thirty nine?"

"Sure as hell is."

"I thought that was right. Well, how would you feel about being the weekend lookout? Only be for a few weekends. I thought it might be a hell of an idea."

"It sure is, Sherman."

...

Unlike the last time, a guide hiked up with Samuel to make sure he got there alright. The sight of the tower flooded the old lookout with memories. The seventy eight steps he counted out of long-dormant habit, and greeted the regular lookout with as much civility as he could muster in the moment. He walked immediately to the window and looked out. There was almost nothing to see. It was a foggy day, the clouds coming in close around the tower, blanketing it in, a cloistered box in the sky.

"Hopefully some of this'll burn off this weekend so you can actually see the ridges."

"I know where they are," Samuel said. "And besides, It's already the most beautiful thing I've ever seen."

Made in the USA
Columbia, SC
27 July 2024